Silver Buckles

Grace Gibson

Meryton Press

OYSTERVILLE, WA

◇◇◇

" Gibson crafts her own exquisite twist to Austen's beloved novel, resulting in an utterly delightful, satisfying read."

—Jan Hahn, author of
An Arranged Marriage
and *The Journey*

◇◇◇

ISBN: 978-1-68131-043-5

Cover design by Janet Taylor
Front cover painting: *La Soirée* by Vittorio Reggiannini (1838-1938)
Back Cover painting: *The Ball* (1906) by Charles Wilda [left musician, Johann Strauss; top middle musician (standing), Joseph Lanner]
Book design by Ellen Pickels

Published in the United States of America.

Dedication

For Cynthia Lane, who mentored me throughout 2020 and encouraged me to poke my nose out into the world and do something with my writing.

Chapter 1

Mr. Darcy's Story…   *Meryton Assembly Rooms*

I stood at the edge of a bacchanal. The noise—it could hardly be called music—was pitched to a high screech that emanated from a second-rate gaggle of performers. I loathe a crush, and I do not like to associate with people who are unfamiliar with the word 'dignity.'

Deuce take you, Bingley! I raged inwardly at my host. I was only there because, if I had refused to come, his sister Caroline would have felt obliged to stay home and *entertain* me. Survival, I mused darkly, is sometimes an uncomfortable business.

Somehow, my friend Charles Bingley had sniffed out my location. I stood off to the side of the room, and he came toward me, panting with enthusiasm.

"Come, Darcy," he said joyfully, "I must have you dance. I cannot bear to see you standing about in this stupid manner." He then continued to pressure me and even pointed out the sister of his own most recent partner. "Do let me ask Miss Bennet to introduce you," he said.

"Good lord, Bingley!" I replied impatiently. "I have been paraded before a hundred people tonight and had names babbled at me from every corner of the room. I am certain I am known to *her,* but you will forgive me for failing to distinguish one girl in a white dress from another." And while I reluctantly admitted Bingley's partner was the prettiest girl in the room, the offer of an introduction to her sister smacked of meager leavings, and I had no intention of standing up with anyone that evening.

"She is tolerable, I suppose, but not handsome enough to tempt me," I replied, and then seeing him take a breath to persuade me from my vile mood, I added, "Do go away, Bingley. I am not inclined to give consequence to young ladies who are slighted by other men."

Bingley, whose sunny disposition did not allow him to be vexed, only shrugged and laughed before he left me alone. As I stood there brooding—as he is fond of calling the state of sober silence—I noticed the object of our recent conversation out of the corner of my eye.

She was a dark-haired girl, small and unremarkable. I had responded to Bingley's urgings by rote, knowing after an initial scan of the room that there were no ladies present who could tempt me to the floor, and I was gratified I had not erred in refusing to stand up with her. She was looking out onto the swarm of dancers, seemingly quite engaged in her observations, but then I noticed, as I examined her covertly, that the girl had about her mouth a coy little smirk.

She had heard me!

An unwelcome warmth crawled up my neck. That I spoke with full consciousness I would be overheard I cannot deny, but to see the consequences of an insult so casually delivered left me slightly breath-less. My beastly state notwithstanding, I do have my standards. I limit myself to a hair's breadth above behaving like a lout. And so, I stepped directly up to the young lady—one of the Bennet sisters, I believe, although I must be forgiven for not knowing which one.

"Miss Bennet," I said with a stiff bow, "I believe you may have overheard my ungenerous remark just now."

The lady had slowly risen when she perceived I was about to address her. She held her head proudly, cocked slightly to the side, with her right eyebrow delicately raised. "Sir," she replied in cold acknowledgement.

"Forgive me. My friend Mr. Bingley is unbearably persistent, and I spoke intemperately only to deflect his efforts to force me to enjoy myself." I spoke briskly. I am not one to simper or whine.

There was an archness in her manner as she replied. "You do not like a country dance, I surmise."

I do not know why, but this gambit forced a wry half smile from me. "I do not, Miss Bennet."

"Very well. If your explanation was given as a sort of apology—"

"It was."

"Then I accept your *explanation* and give you leave to return to the wall you have been supporting for the last half an hour."

Never in my life had I been so rudely dismissed! I would be damned to hell if I scuttled away like a scolded child. I held out my hand.

"I believe, Miss Bennet, we had better dance. It would look odd for us to have stood here in conversation for as long as we have without ending our tête-à-tête in the usual manner."

"But you abhor dancing, Mr. Darcy," she said gravely, and for a second, I thought she might even refuse!

"I have never said so. I abhor being urged to dance as though I only require a nudge. Come, I am standing here with my hand extended, and we are now creating a scene."

A reluctant grin threatened to undo Miss Bennet's smoldering glare, and she took my hand.

Elizabeth's Story...

I TOOK MY PLACE IN THE LINE OF DANCERS WITH MR. DARCY. EGAD, the man was insufferable, but this was the most fun I had had in ages! He looked pinched and irritated, but to be fair, he made a very elegant partner. How could I resist teasing him just a little?

"You are not the only one in your party who does not enjoy a country dance, I think, sir," I remarked as we swirled past Mr. Bingley's two sisters and his brother-in-law. The three of them stared at us with expressions of dismay.

My partner offered a tight, mirthless smile. I thought he might be silent for the rest of the dance, but then he abruptly replied, "I cannot imagine why they do not rejoice at being jostled, observed, and discussed like fairground curiosities."

I laughed at him.

"*You*," he said pointedly, "enjoy this vulgar romp, do you?"

"*I* am not above my company."

He seemed to ruminate as the steps of the dance separated us, but when he once again took up my hand, he was ready with a most provoking rejoinder.

"What *is* that noise?" he asked plaintively.

We had just rounded the corner of the room where my mother loudly held court. I sensed we were to take the buttons off our foils and fence in earnest now.

"Oh!" I replied brightly, "that is my mother. I am dancing with the richest man in Derbyshire, and she is planning our wedding."

This startled a bark of laughter from Mr. Darcy-of-ten-thousand-a-year. "And just how do you plan to secure me, Miss—forgive me, I do not recall which of the dozen unmarried Bennet sisters I have the pleasure of entertaining."

"I am Miss Elizabeth, sir. Our hovel is just over three miles from the palace of Netherfield. You might see me pulling turnips from the garden if you pass that way tomorrow."

For the first time, Mr. Darcy looked at me in earnest. I did not get the impression he was entirely displeased with what he saw, so I pressed my advantage. "But you really should not laugh at my teasing, sir."

"Why not?" he asked with a tiny frown.

"Because your friends seem quite put out that you are enjoying

8

yourself. I believe, if they raise their noses any higher in the air, we shall see right into their skulls."

"They *are* above their company," the deplorable man replied as though he offered a reasonable defense for snobbery.

"Oh? They are saints and angels, then? My word, how fortunate we heathens of Hertfordshire are tonight."

My partner visibly relaxed, and a genuine smile flashed toward me for the briefest second. "Well," he admitted, "I believe Mr. Hurst *is* a saint. He is forever in their company, yet he bears up regardless."

"I see the saint is taking Communion now," I replied with a twinkling laugh. As one, we turned to watch him at the refreshments table, drinking down the contents of a glass in one gulp and reaching for a second.

"Yes, he is devoted to his bread and wine." We watched in amusement as he piled his plate high with shaved ham and local cheeses.

"And his hair shirt?"

"He is married to it," my partner replied.

It was my turn to laugh aloud. If I continued in this vein, I would be no better than my sister Lydia who, at this juncture, was roaring at something John Lucas was telling her. My unladylike whoop of laughter caused Mr. Bingley's sisters to look, if it were possible, even more outraged than before.

Upon rejoining after the *chaine anglaise* had temporarily separated us, Mr. Darcy followed my gaze, which was still aimed at Mr. Bingley's sisters, and he said in a musing way, "Ah. As I suspected."

"What is as you suspected, sir?"

"Their noses are held so high I can clearly see their skulls are indeed hollow as gourds," he replied quietly and close to my ear.

"Angels are not known for their intelligence," I explained sweetly.

"No," he replied with a smile. Was he admiring *my* intelligence?

Sadly, the strains of the dance were ending, and with surprising reluctance, I followed Mr. Darcy off the floor.

Before we parted, he said, "If you are sitting down for the last set—"

"Do you mean if I continue to be slighted by other men?"

"Yes. If you are without a partner at the end of the evening, I shall lend you my consequence by leading you out again, Miss Elizabeth."

Mr. Darcy's Story…

I HAD DONE SOMETHING I NEVER DO. I HAD ASKED A MARRIAGEABLE young lady for a second dance. For the first time since I had engaged this surprising country girl in a game of wits, Miss Elizabeth sobered.

"We must not stand up again, Mr. Darcy," she said in a shy voice.

"We must not?" Was that a tinge of wheedling in my voice? Good lord!

"My mother will indeed remark on it, sir, and make my life unbearable." With that, she looked downward, and I saw her dark lashes rest on her pinking cheeks and felt myself quite sympathetic to the chit.

"Well then," I said in a gentle murmur low enough only for her to hear, "I shall look for you in the turnip patch in the morning. We have hardly begun to make sport of all our acquaintances." Elizabeth Bennet looked up and blinded me with a smile I shall not soon forget.

So, this is a flirtation! I marveled. I had heard many a man wax poetically on the merits of such a playful and dangerous game, but I never knew what the fuss was about.

I spent the rest of the evening in a pleasant cocoon. I had never been easy in the company of marriageable ladies because I am an acknowledged catch. But this one, this Miss Elizabeth Bennet, was fair game. She made it clear to me somehow that she was not the *catching* sort. She could endure my attentions without her expectations being raised, and the echoes of our testy, jesting dance floor match reverberated delightfully in my mind.

BEFORE I KNEW IT, MY PARTY WAS IN THE CARRIAGE RETURNING TO Bingley's leased estate, Netherfield Park. My pleasant reflections could not be penetrated, even by the sharp criticisms of Bingley's sisters.

Caroline Bingley, in particular, was waspish that evening as we gathered in the salon. She had a great deal to say about the horrible quality of the company, her mortification at being required to be civil to such mushrooms, and the shabbiness of the Bennet daughters' attire.

Bingley took up a good-natured defense of Miss Jane Bennet, the eldest. She was an angel, he insisted, and inwardly I laughed. Her sister Elizabeth was definitely *not* an angel.

Miss Bingley, believing herself to be crafty, appeased her brother by acknowledging that Miss Bennet was a pretty and pleasant sort of girl, but the mother and the younger sisters—deplorable hoydens! And she heard that Miss Elizabeth was thought to be nearly as handsome as Miss Bennet.

"Hardly," Miss Bingley sniffed and slanted her eyes at me.

I continued to smile blandly at all that was said. Miss Elizabeth did not need me to defend her against the likes of a Miss Bingley. Of course, I was the first to retire for the night, and I spent the rest of the week riding along the road to Mr. Bennet's estate, Longbourn, in hopes of accidentally meeting my new flirt.

As with every expert temptress, Miss Elizabeth was elusive. I saw her once on a parallel track, her petticoats flashing as she walked briskly up and over a rise. I shall own to a jolt of surprise because never in my life had I seen a woman truly *walk*. They toddled or minced along, or in the case of those serving pints in a tavern, dashed about in a helter-skelter rush.

Two weeks passed, and I still had not had the satisfaction of meeting Miss Elizabeth again. Certainly, there had been a few sightings—hat tipping and a bobbing curtsey in Meryton and again after church services. At last, however, our party was invited to Lucas Lodge, and from the buoyancy and exuberance of my friend Bingley, I surmised that he had been assured the Bennets would be in attendance.

Lucas Lodge

AN AFTERNOON AT A COUNTRY HOUSE FILLED WITH STRANGERS WHO are neither elegant nor dignified is a kind of torture for me. Moreover, these people have known each other all their lives, and they are so comfortable together that one is acutely aware of being an outsider. Miss Bingley attempted to commiserate with me as I stood awkwardly on the fringes of the melee. I was having none of it, answering in a dead, mechanical voice to all her lamentations while watching the doorway for the Bennets.

When Miss Elizabeth entered the room, I left Miss Bingley and went directly to my object.

"Mr. Darcy!" she exclaimed in mild surprise at my undisguised eagerness to greet her. "You seem in high spirits. I had not thought this sort of gathering would be to your taste. I came fully prepared to witness your silent indignation at such a mode of passing an evening."

"Yes, but I have thought that this middling sort of entertainment would be delightful to you. Am I right?"

"Well, when one lives in drudgery while plotting how to marry well, these *middling entertainments* as you call them are a respite." Just as I opened my mouth to reply, she turned to greet Miss Lucas. "Oh, Charlotte, how pretty you look! Excuse me, Mr. Darcy, but I believe Mrs. Long is trying to get my attention."

Dismissed! Delightful girl! I was sure a lazy smile threatened to give me away at that moment, and so I found a window and looked out at a mediocre garden while Miss Elizabeth's middle sister—the plain one—plunked away at the pianoforte.

Miss Bingley was sure to trap me there for the purpose of more commiseration on such horrid playing however, so I looked around for an alternative and encountered my host, Sir William Lucas. He was a garrulous and amiable man, benevolent and believing himself to be quite an important figure after having been tapped on the shoulder by the King. He was not in any way an elegant or intelligent man, and he spoke endlessly of his brief moment in the sun at St. James's Palace. However, just as I was about to snub him as he droned on in a most insufferable way, I caught the eye of Miss Elizabeth.

She was evaluating me, poised to judge me as I spoke to Sir William. She glanced softly at the man I was about to skewer with some pithy remark, and I pulled up short. Did she indeed like this oaf? Well, he was a harmless sort; I could grant her that at least. I took a deep breath and began to converse with a bit more consideration for someone who was trying desperately to earn my approbation. With one eye on my host and one eye on my saucy monitor, I listened to the minute details of a room at the palace where Sir William was honored—a second-rate chamber if I recall, used to dispatch the hordes of persons singled out for a token aimed solely at keeping the mythology of the Liege Lord intact.

I expected a reward, and what I received was a most dissatisfying afternoon in which I tried desperately to put myself in a position to earn it. Finally, at the very end of the ordeal, I pinned down my quarry only to receive a pert sort of farewell.

Chapter 2

Feeling slightly abused—well, to be honest, I was feeling *horribly ill-used*—I strove to get on with the business at hand. I had come to Hertfordshire to help Bingley with his first estate, albeit a leased one, and to give him a rudimentary education on what is expected should he indeed purchase a property. Mr. Hurst only roused himself to shoot birds or to sit down to a meal, and our mornings were consequently spent in the former activity. The afternoons were taken up with the steward, surveys of the land, casual meetings with tenant farmers, and a frustrating attempt on my part to capture Bingley's attention.

"If you purchase this place, Bingley, you will have to do something about the home farm."

"Hmm?"

"It is in a deplorable state. Did you not remark in what an outdated way the harvest is planned?"

"Oh...well. I suppose. Is it? What do you recommend?"

As we trudged along, I became more irritable by the minute. Finally, I blurted out what I was thinking. "Let us suspend our conference for now. Your mind is not even in the room."

"What? Oh. I suppose not. I say, Darcy, I have accepted an invitation to dine with the officers tomorrow afternoon."

"What officers?"

"Colonel Forster and his lieutenants. The militia is encamped outside Meryton for the winter. You and Hurst will join me, will you not?"

I could hardly stay back and read in front of the fire. With such a temptation as my fortune, Miss Bingley would find a way to fall into my lap in a theatrical swoon, and her equally calculating sister would find a way to absent herself until she burst in upon our *embrace*.

While inwardly tallying the number of days remaining in my holiday, I agreed to go along, but the next morning I found myself unequal to another moment sitting attendance on Bingley's family. Nor did I seek out the vixen from Longbourn. She was too sly for me by half. Instead, I called for my horse and turned up the road away from Meryton, heading for a hill the residents called Oakham.

Along the way I thought of my sister. I should not have been in Hertfordshire at all. In truth, I was avoiding Georgiana because I was at a loss with regards to the inner workings of a girl of sixteen. Her life had been almost completely ruined, having been nearly seduced into a disastrous elopement by a fortune hunter. Time, I hoped, would do for her what I could not.

Perfectly caught up in this unhappy train of thought, I topped the rise and startled a young lady sitting alone on a fallen log overlooking the valley that spread out like a cottager's quilt in shades of gold and red.

"Mr. Darcy!"

"Miss Elizabeth!"

We were equally surprised and uncomfortable. To meet alone in this way was not without its risks. As one, we looked at the road behind me to make sure we had not been caught.

"Few people come here, sir." She looked at me as though she expected me to bid her 'good day' and continue down the other side of the hill.

Perhaps it was only the shaded nature of my own thoughts that morning that led me to notice her shadowed eyes and a demure quality to her posture that I had not yet seen. Something troubled her, and at once I was on the ground and tethering my horse to a sapling near the verge.

"But where is your fire this morning? You normally do not greet me with such reluctance. Are you not eager to put me in my place today?" I spoke with the intention of goading her, of rousing her to resume our flirtation.

She mustered a half smile and floundered for a reply. "Ah, well," she said weakly, "you have caught me in a rare moment of self-doubt. Do your worst, and snub me creditably."

Her vulnerability alarmed me. "I shall do so, certainly, but first you must tell me what ails you. Are you ill?"

She chuckled softly. "Yes. Yes, I am so ill I have walked two miles up this mountain."

"Very well," I said reasonably, but in truth I was slightly nettled. "Do not tell me what has robbed you of your spark. I shall take my leave of you." I said this without any intention of going away, and it worked predictably.

"You are not in spirits yourself," she said in an almost biting tone. "Shall I pry and ask you whether you are ill? Do you have a headache? Are your affairs in disarray? Has your family caused you vexation?"

Her last remark was near enough to the truth, and I sucked in my breath involuntarily. "Very well. Gloves off, I take it? As a matter of fact, my life is not all comfort and ease."

"You surprise me. I had thought that having the ready means to do almost anything in the world, to be secure, and to have the freedom you surely have would be sufficient to deflect almost every difficulty."

She was dangerously close to provoking me in earnest, and I said in all seriousness, "You are not alone. I have troubles too."

I would have turned to go then, but she averted her gaze very sharply, and I suspected she was swallowing tears. I held my breath.

"You may as well know because you will learn it soon enough. You are to dine with the officers this evening, are you not?"

"Yes."

"Mr. Bingley's sisters have invited my sister Jane to dine with them while you are away."

"Oh? And how is this a matter that requires you to seek the solace of Oakham Mount?"

Her hesitation alarmed me, and I took a step toward her.

"My mother has insisted that Jane ride to Netherfield this afternoon, although those clouds coming from the east will surely bring on a hard rain."

"Can she not take the carriage?"

"My mother forbids it, and my father only laughs." In response to my frown of confusion she added, "Mama hopes it will rain and force my sister to stay the night."

"To catch Bingley," I said. My tone was now grim. I despise a fortune hunter.

Miss Elizabeth protested a little sharply at the implication of my displeasure. "To attach him certainly is my *mother's* aim, but Jane would never compromise her reputation, I assure you."

I looked out at the bank of clouds that had caused her such dismay. "We had better turn back if we are not to be soaked ourselves. May I walk with you?"

"You need not be obliged, Mr. Darcy. I am a strong walker and go everywhere alone."

"Surely, that does not preclude the reasonableness of my company. I must travel the same road after all, and I detest riding away from a lady who must cough in my dust."

We walked along for about half a mile in silence. She is indeed a strong walker. I never once felt compelled to adjust my stride.

"Is your mother truly so determined to find husbands for her daughters?" I asked.

"Our estate is a two-thousand-a-year affair, entailed upon a cousin we have never met."

"Ah."

"Ah, indeed. There are no dowries to speak of for my sisters and me. My mother believes she will outlive Papa and end her days in the hedgerows."

I deplore hyperbole. "Perhaps not the hedgerows."

"No, of course not. But she will no longer be the mistress of a property, nor will she have the luxuries she is used to or have the standing upon which she relies to feel comfortable. My father, bless him, certainly does nothing to support her feelings of self-worth."

"Is it really so very bad?"

"I believe it is. However, I cannot imagine Jane shrinking into ignoble spinsterhood. She is too beautiful…too good. Someone will love her, and I shall not repine for the rest of us. We shall do, I assure you."

"Of course you shall," I said, angling a pointed look at her.

"No," she said crossly. "Do not infer upon me some quality of stoutheartedness. I am not the admirable sort. If the worst comes to pass, I shall weather it well only because I am stubborn."

I smiled at her. "That I do not doubt. But what time will your sister leave for Netherfield?"

"Within the hour, I think."

"Then I have time. If you will excuse me." I pulled my horse forward and stepped into the stirrup. Then I tipped my hat and left the lady on the road, choking in my dust.

Chapter 3

Elizabeth's Story...

What a perplexing man! Mr. Darcy was fast becoming an object of fascination to me, and I hated to be at his mercy. How could I have unbent and confessed that my mother schemes in a humiliating way? I walked along—stormed along more like—trying to decide what maggot possessed me to display such weakness. Finally, I reached a state of glum acceptance.

I told Mr. Darcy because he would very soon know it. Jane would arrive at Netherfield, soaked to the skin, and very naturally be asked to shelter for the night, and Mr. Darcy would hear the whole sordid tale from Caroline Bingley over breakfast.

At least I had given him the reason for such an abhorrent display, and hopefully, he would not hold Jane to blame for the machinations of my mother. I knew Mr. Darcy to be a man of the world and expected him to recognize that my mother acted out of fear and not greed. Desperate people do desperate things.

My marching pace delivered me to Longbourn in time to see an elegant coach drawn up to the door.

"But what is this?" I asked Kitty, who stood in open-mouthed wonder on the steps.

"Mr. Darcy has sent his coach for Jane with his compliments."

I, too, stood with my jaw hanging open. My mother came out all in a fluster. She was not sure whether she should be annoyed that her plans had gone awry or overjoyed that a rich man paid this mark of attention to her most beautiful daughter. Either way, Jane stepped into the coach, which delivered her safely, to return later that evening in the same style.

Of her dinner with Mr. Bingley's sisters, Jane only said it was pleasant. But once we retired, she quietly confessed to having been interrogated as though by inquisitors.

"They were very kind," she said quietly.

"But they demanded to know all about your connections."

"Yes, Lizzy."

"And they gleefully heard of your uncle in trade and your uncle who is a Meryton solicitor."

Jane nodded in the candlelight.

"And they also know of the entail? Did they have the gall to ask you to name the sum of your dowry?"

"No," Jane replied sadly.

"But they will already know we have only a thousand pounds from our mother's portion and that only payable upon her passing. These things are easy to find out, and those two seem well suited to such indelicate inquiries when their brother takes an interest in a lady."

"Lizzy!"

"Do you believe their interest is kindly motivated? If so, you are more naïve than I thought."

After a long silence, Jane said, "Miss Bingley was a little put out that Mr. Darcy sent his coach for me."

"And so she made sure you felt the sting of her vexation."

"I can no longer believe she is sincere in her friendship." Jane looked abstractedly at her image in the mirror. "Now, let us leave this conversation behind us. I am for bed, my dear."

My sister kissed my forehead, and I braided her hair before she slipped quietly into bed. The very air around her spoke of her disappointment. She knew Mr. Bingley would be told he must not think of marrying such a disadvantaged girl, and she was too modest to hope her character would have more value to the man than her connections and her paltry dowry.

At least Mr. Darcy had salvaged my family's reputation a little by thwarting Mama's scheme. For all his superiority and intolerance for those he perceives to be beneath his notice, I began to think Mr. Darcy might be a man capable of consideration. And he delighted me with his enraging provocations.

Are you ill?—indeed! What a ludicrous thing to say to a person!

Mr. Darcy's Story…

Bingley continued to be smitten by the eldest Bennet daughter. I continued to be fascinated by the second. But in all earnestness, neither of us could have any real ambitions in this vein.

After Bingley's sisters hosted Miss Bennet, we heard repeatedly of the unsuitability of that family. Their deplorable connections did indeed daunt me, but their lack of fortune, at least, I already knew. If only this news were enough to harass me—but no, I was not to be left alone. Miss Bingley did not like me sending a carriage to Longbourn, and she made sure I was aware I had displeased her.

"Jane Bennet will let this small attention go to her head, sir," Miss Bingley said.

"Hmm."

We walked in the shrubbery on a drizzly afternoon. I had escaped the house in search of air, only to be stalked and pounced upon in a moment of abstraction.

"Assure me, Mr. Darcy, that you will consider the appearance of things in future. For you, the offer of a carriage is nothing."

Not 'nothing.' I made a statement to be sure but not the one you suspect. I did not utter this reply aloud, but I thought it with a measure of alarming satisfaction.

Miss Bingley did not wait for me to reply and continued to remonstrate with me. "For such an impoverished girl, the arrival of your coach must have signaled you are enamored at the least."

Yes, at the very least I am enamored, I silently replied. However, this observation warned me I had better proceed with caution.

This flirtation with Miss Elizabeth had begun to threaten my better judgment. I felt more than a little reckless when I thought of her. I am not practiced in the art of dalliance and wondered whether perhaps I should quit the field. And I might very well have left beforehand were it not for two things.

First, who should arrive in Meryton but my archenemy and my sister's would-be seducer—George Wickham! I had to refrain from growling aloud at the mere mention of his name. And secondly, Bingley had decided to give a ball. I meant to be there if only to make sure Wickham stayed away. He would not dare show his face anywhere I happened to be. And, if I were to stay a little while longer, I was determined to be more circumspect with regards to the dark-haired lady from Longbourn.

Chapter 4

Elizabeth's Story…

I did not see Mr. Darcy for two weeks together. Mr. Bingley called regularly, and though he seemed amenable, he had yet to be wrangled by my mother into sitting down for a family dinner. She was thoroughly frustrated, therefore, by his refusal to engage himself promptly to Jane, and I do believe she would have planned desperate measures were it not for the arrival of another marriageable prospect: Mr. William Collins.

Mr. Collins is my father's heir. We had never met him, but he arrived cloaked in dignity, having sent a letter to Papa saying that he is a rector, holds a tidy living under the patronage of a baroness, and intends to marry one of us to negate the injury of the entail, which he holds through no fault of his own. I would have been much inclined to like him because such a gesture is the mark of a man who at least has some sort of conscience, but in fact, Mr. Collins is a dolt.

The man is a simpering idiot! That he could read scriptures and deliver a homily struck me as a conundrum until we learned that his patroness, Lady Catherine de Bourgh, tells him what to say.

And what should be his pleasure with regards to his future, but to marry me! I was slightly amused and thoroughly appalled. Jane would likely have been his first choice, but Mama put him off with hints that she would soon be engaged to Mr. Bingley. This was an exaggeration, but I was glad Jane would be spared Mr. Collins's attentions. I thought Mary might willingly have our cousin because she was too pious to notice his stupidity. But given a few years, she would see that her husband was a dogmatic imbecile. No, I could not wish him on any one of us.

Reduced to hiding in my own home, I took to escaping out the kitchen door in all kinds of weather to avoid the dreadful man's attentions. The day before the Netherfield ball—a vexatious source of upheaval in itself!—I ducked out of the hall and marched away before I could be caught by Mama and chained to my needlework. I left with only my cloak and put my hood up to keep from getting drenched, but soon enough, though it was only drizzling, I was wet to the skin. I headed to my Aunt Philips's house, and there I met Mr. George Wickham.

I arrived in a dampened state, and after a hasty adjustment in front of the hallway mirror, I styled my hair in the simplest knot, and yet Mr. Wickham managed, in the space of a moment, to make me feel as though I were the most beautiful woman in the room. What a charmer! My mind, having lately been filled with the idiocy of Mr. Collins and the arrogance of Mr. Darcy, could not help but compare my new acquaintance with them.

Intelligently conversant, polished, and subtle in the delivery of compliments, Mr. Wickham was a welcome antidote to William Collins, who soon appeared with his umbrella and my younger sisters in tow. Mr. Collins, by following me around like a dog, showed he had come to find me. My sisters, by bursting into the room in romping high spirits, showed they had come to find officers. Aunt Philips's house was open every afternoon for card parties, and on a drizzly day, there was no other entertainment on offer in Meryton. Thus, we were all assembled quite by accident.

Mr. Wickham, being perceptive, soon came to my aid and did what he could to thwart the attentions of my cousin. If I sat on the settee, Mr. Wickham appeared instantly to fill the seat next to me, leaving Mr. Collins in the position of pacing in front of me and expounding on the merits of his situation and religious views. My aunt proved helpful by corralling the man toward a card game where he played so poorly he disgusted everybody.

Meanwhile, the newly commissioned officer I was quickly coming to esteem engaged me in conversation. His manners continued to be gentle. He showed himself to be agreeable, determined to be pleasant, and thus Mr. Wickham appeared to me to be the antithesis of Mr. Darcy. Having just thought of that man, I was quite astonished when Mr. Wickham mentioned he had grown up at Pemberley.

"You know Mr. Darcy, then?" I asked in surprise.

He related that they had grown up and were educated together, and as the son of old Mr. Darcy's steward, he was favored and singled out for distinction. As this tidbit unraveled, my curiosity grew by leaps and bounds. I cajoled and encouraged Mr. Wickham, who demonstrated appropriate reluctance, to say more. Of Mr. Darcy, I noted, he would not speak without a hesitant sort of care.

He glanced sideways at me as though trying to determine my opinion of the man before he could be candid. Eventually, he asked, "Is Mr. Darcy well thought of in this neighborhood?"

"He is certainly thought of," I said with a vicious twinkle, for I thought of him almost constantly! "But the general opinion is that he is above his company. Do you find him otherwise?" I asked demurely.

"I wish I could say Mr. Darcy is the most agreeable man of my acquaintance, but in truth, he is fastidious and proud and at times a most hardened character."

"Hardened?" I exclaimed. Certainly, Mr. Darcy enjoyed crossing swords with me, and that was hardly the mode of a gentleman, and I had seen him struggle against his annoyance and disgust when forced to be in our country society. "I have seen his pride and the arrogance natural to a rich, powerful man, but you hint at a shade in his character I have not seen. What has he done to give you such an opinion of him?"

Mr. Wickham smiled at me, an expression ingenious for its sympathy for my naiveté, and clear in his intention to allow me the comfort of my delusions.

"Let us talk of pleasanter things," he replied lightly.

But I would not allow it. In the space of five minutes, I had the whole of his story. I believed him. Of course I believed him! How could I not when the details were all neatly in place?

The late Mr. Darcy had favored the young man, and in his will, set out to provide him with a valuable living and even engaged to educate him for the church. But before this happy plan could be enacted, the old man died unexpectedly, and his heir, the Mr. Darcy of the penetrating stare and blunt assessments, had denied Mr. Wickham his due.

"But I do not repine," Mr. Wickham said sweetly. He was a master at looking the picture of a disappointed man determined to be cheerful, and it was this that caused me the first inkling of unease. "I have my new career," he went on soulfully, "and I mean to do well at it. And, with society such as this—new friends and acquaintances so very agreeable—I count myself fortunate indeed."

This was all very shocking, and I hardly knew what to think, but there was something slightly chafing about Mr. Wickham's story. Indeed, after my first inclination to swallow his tale whole, I classed it as a story rather than the absolute truth, and I would have picked at him very gently to unravel his assertions if Mr. Collins at that moment had not looked to be standing up from the card table. Quick as a flash, I absconded, and expecting to be hunted down by my odious cousin, I went home the long way around through Mrs. Long's garden, across fallow fields, over stiles, and through a dry creek bed.

Triumph and cleverness came with a consequence, however, for when I happened to glance behind me, whom should I see but Mr. Collins in the distance, waving and struggling to reach me. I dashed ahead and crossed over the road to Netherfield to cut through a hedge, but in my haste, I stepped on a loose stone and fell in a flash of pain. I had twisted an ankle!

I sat on the edge of the road in a disheveled mound of dampened cloak and dusty hems, clutching my throbbing ankle, when Mr. Darcy appeared atop a great tall horse over the rise of a hill.

He dismounted instantly and came to me. "Miss Elizabeth, what has happened? Are you well?"

The full impact of the impression I made fell on me. With what humiliation did I undergo his interrogation and his unapologetic examination of my ankle. I blushed at the condition of my walking boots—scuffed and now muddy—with dull, tarnished brass buckles holding tight my well-worn straps. Blushing and stammering, I sought to make him go away, insisting I would be well enough to continue in a minute. But no! He would stand there and continue to wonder what had happened.

"Indeed, sir. It was nothing. I only slipped on a loose stone."

"But I have seen you walking, and I cannot believe you would not be able to catch yourself from falling. A more sure-footed young lady I have never met."

I looked obliquely behind him. My cousin was now within hailing distance and would soon bear down upon me.

Mr. Darcy, quick to notice everything, followed my gaze. "Who is that? Is that man following you? Were you running from him?"

Looking up into my interlocutor's eyes, I smiled a bit grimly. "*That* sir, is the man my mother intends me to marry."

"What? But who is this person?" he demanded.

"He is none other than my cousin, the man who will inherit Longbourn. And, having been incapacitated on the road here, I begin to know what a wounded animal must feel as the hunter approaches."

By this time, Mr. Collins was upon us, red-faced, gasping for air, irritated, and astounded to find me down in the dirt.

"Cousin, you should not be walking out alone. I forbid it!" he roared. "Did you not hear me calling you to return to me? And you, sir," he cried upon noticing I was not alone, "who are you?"

Mr. Darcy replied very coldly. "Who are *you*, sir? This lady is known to me, and I am here to offer her aid. She has injured her ankle." He then very determinedly and pointedly turned his back on Mr. Collins. "Are you able to stand? Let me help you."

He supported me as I stood with my weight on one leg. Mr. Collins began to sputter his objections, and Mr. Darcy said in a voice loud enough to overcome his protest, "I shall put you on my horse and have you home in no time at all."

I would have objected—*violently* objected—in other circumstances. I am not a horsewoman, and above all things I hate being treated like a fragile trinket. I have twisted my ankle before. It is a hazard of walking all one's life, and I have limped home without incident. But Mr. Collins's presence was so abhorrent at that mortifying moment that I welcomed Mr. Darcy's intervention and let him lift me up on his steed.

Perched precariously sideways and gripping the saddle, I am sure my eyes showed my misgivings to my rescuer, but he would have none of my missishness.

"Hold tight and try to relax," he said impatiently as he walked to the side, holding the reins. "We have only a mile or so to go."

Soon, we were plodding down the road. Meanwhile, Mr. Collins buzzed around us like a gnat. He appeared shocked, appalled, and dismayed—certain some impropriety was occurring right under his nose.

"I demand to know who you are, sir," he said.

"You demand, do you?" Mr. Darcy said crisply. He looked perfectly dangerous to my eyes, and were I Mr. Collins, I would have stepped back. Things were bad enough without bloodshed, I thought. Tight-lipped with pain and unnerved by Mr. Darcy's very tall horse, I intervened.

"Cousin, allow me to introduce Mr. Darcy of Pemberley. Mr. Collins, you understand, sir, is visiting. He is a rector in Kent."

"Mr. Darcy! But you must be nephew to my patroness, Lady Catherine de Bourgh. But how gracious of you to help my cousin Elizabeth! Such a naughty puss for running from me, but we shall have her set to rights in no time."

I looked down at Mr. Darcy who stared straight ahead with narrowed eyes and a clenched jaw. "Try to relax," I murmured. "We have only a mile or so to go."

Mr. Darcy endeavored not to smile at my repetition of his earlier assurance and continued stoically down the road, but my cousin would not let us proceed in peace. Having sniffed out a man of consequence, he now sang an entirely different tune from his initial outrage. For an interminable space of time, he talked uninterruptedly. He was overjoyed to be acquainted with Mr. Darcy, delighted to share his multiple observations of Lady Catherine's excellence and completely disinterested in me, the companion of his future life. After what felt to be an hour but was more rightly about four minutes, Mr. Darcy halted our progress.

"Mr. Collins, do run ahead to Longbourn and tell Mrs. Bennet that her daughter has sprained her ankle," he said in a tone I am sure he would use with a footman. "Perhaps she will engage you to ride into Meryton for a doctor."

"Of course! Of course!" my cousin cried. And without thinking, he lumbered away from us.

Mr. Darcy kept his horse at a stand until Mr. Collins was out of sight. "Will you marry that man?" he asked me, incredulous.

"I would sooner run away with the tinker."

"Can your mother force you to it?"

"My father certainly can. If he invokes upon me the burden of duty, I am afraid I would have to sacrifice myself."

"Surely, if you object, he will not do so."

"My father is an indifferent parent. He often concedes to my mother because he dislikes her hysterics. But in this case, I believe he will be selfish."

Mr. Darcy looked up at me sharply. Was that distress I saw in his face? Surely not. Nevertheless, I gave in to the impulse to reassure him.

"He will not force me because he could not stand to have that simpleton underfoot. Mr. Collins has been an amusing character to Papa, but his considerable appreciation for the diversion he has created is beginning to flag. No, I am sure he will allow my refusal to stand, but oh, how I dread such a proposal!"

Mr. Darcy began to walk again at the slowest pace possible. Eventually, he introduced a different subject altogether. He seemed prone to speaking without preamble.

"Your episode today will prevent the pleasure of my dancing with you tomorrow."

My ankle throbbed; else, I would have laughed at him. Instead, I said, "You assume dancing with you is a pleasure?"

"I referred to my own pleasure at dancing with *you*, but I believe you choose to willfully misunderstand me."

"Well then, how stupid of me to willfully interrupt your pleasure!"

A sardonic half smile peeked out, and he replied very lightly, "Exactly so. We men of wealth and privilege are not inclined to be denied. I shall, if I may, engage you to sit out the first dance with me."

"How delightful! We shall select a very good wall to uphold. You will stand there, righteously indignant at the vulgarity of Hertfordshire society, I shall sit wretchedly beside you, wishing I could be out there with the rabble, and together we shall watch the enjoyment of others while provoking one another."

"I certainly hope so," he said. And then in a tone that was very nearly tender he asked, "Are you in pain?"

I looked down at him, and he looked up at me. Something invisible passed between us that caused my heart to begin racing.

"Mr. Darcy," I said firmly, "you need not change tack and become all consideration. You have demeaned yourself enough today as it is."

"Precisely how have I demeaned myself?"

"You saw with your own eyes that I do not have silver buckles on my shoes," I said in a light jest. "Country damsels are hardly worth *your* gallantry, sir."

He chuckled delightfully. "No? Shall I instead scold you for walking at an indecorous pace? Should I upbraid you for ignoring the dictates of propriety? You should have been in the company of a maid with an umbrella over your head and a handkerchief gently held to your lips to keep you from inhaling the damp. And most certainly, you should not have been scampering about like a boy of fifteen."

"I am sure you should lecture me, sir, but I shall hear plenty of that from my mother. Tell me, instead, of this animal on which I sit. Is he as frightful a beast as I think him to be?"

Chapter 5

Mr. Darcy's Story...

On the evening of the Netherfield ball, as my valet held out my white satin waistcoat, I noticed a strange expression on his face. Having known the man for half my life and believing I had never met a more discreet individual, I was on the verge of a testy inquiry as to the reason for his smirk when I realized I had been whistling a jaunty tune. I am not and have never been a whistler. I straightened my lips into a slash across my face and no longer wondered why he was stifling a chuckle.

"Apparently, I am in high spirits this evening, Carsten," I said, intending to minimize my embarrassment with a dignified statement.

"Apparently so, sir." His eyes met mine for just an instant.

When I was turned out to my valet's satisfaction, I examined myself in the mirror and thought perhaps he had done a little more than his usual polish.

"Very good, Carsten. I think I shall do. Is it safe?"

He stepped out into the hall and looked up and down to make sure Miss Bingley was not loitering in a doorway and hoping to latch on to me for the evening. When I received his nod of assurance, I went down the stairs. We had timed our course of action to the second. Just as I arrived in the foyer, the Bingleys and Hursts came out of the salon and stood ready to receive the guests who arrived in a steady stream.

I do not care for country society overmuch, but I shall own to their excellence in one thing: they arrive at a ball on time. None of the fashionable hour-and-a-half late entrances for these people. They valued their entertainments too much to be cavalier.

I relied on Mrs. Bennet to be one of the first to arrive, and indeed, she was, dressed like a draper's display and stacked from head to toe with lace, flounces, feathers, and a fan. Behind her stood Mr. Bennet who, after extending a weary bow, wandered off to the card room. While the matron of the family held up the progress of half the neighborhood by prattling at Bingley, her youngest girls dipped their curtseys and swarmed into the ballroom. Her middle daughter drifted toward the musicians with an expression of long-suffering, and Bingley, oblivious to the obligations of a good host, swept away the eldest Miss Bennet to ask her opinion of the ballroom's decoration.

All of these movements left Miss Elizabeth to fend for herself, and I went straight down the stairs to her and offered my arm.

"But where is your beau, Miss Elizabeth? I would have thought he would lend you his arm at least."

"Oh, he is quite put out with me, sir. I am being punished, I believe."

"I am sure you deserve it for your antics of yesterday," I said with false severity.

Striving not to appear amused by my teasing, she replied, "That may be, but I have caused a new offence."

"Oh? My word, were you a—what did he call you?—a 'naughty puss,' I believe."

She looked genuinely annoyed to be reminded of Mr. Collins's demeaning scold but obliged me by explaining why I had her company to myself.

"I am incapable of dancing the first set with him."

"Then I can sympathize, for I have been similarly disappointed in you. Is he sulking in a corner?"

She looked up at me with a sudden smile. "He ran off to find my friend Charlotte Lucas in hopes that *she* will do for him what I cannot."

"Poor lady. But how is your fetlock? You are limping less than I expected."

She lowered her voice as we headed for the edge of the room at a stately pace. "If you must know, it hurts very much. For the sake of all our vanities, Mama insisted I take off Mr. Jones's ugly bandage, which leaves the joint unsupported. But I am too proud to wince and hobble in front of my friends."

"Well, if it is any consolation, you look perfectly tolerable tonight."

"Do I indeed? It seems I have been elevated from *merely* tolerable to *perfectly* tolerable. How fortunate I am!"

She chuckled that low and honeyed sound of seduction, and I felt sure of an enjoyable evening. But just when I was about to settle her into a satin-upholstered Queen Anne chair and begin to flirt in earnest, Miss Bingley appeared.

She had upon her face an expression of fixed brightness and a keen, almost martial light in her eye. "Mr. Darcy," she said sweetly before turning a wee bit forced. "Oh, and Eliza Bennet too. Goodness! I did not see you there. I understand you are injured and will not be dancing tonight."

"I shall not have that pleasure, Miss Bingley."

"Well, you had best settle yourself there, I think. I shall have a footman bring you a cup of punch."

Having dismissed her rival, she turned to me and said, "The musicians will start up for the opening dance any minute now."

"Will they?" I asked blandly.

"Yes. We open with the cotillion, as most elegant balls usually do. *You* dance the cotillion very creditably, Mr. Darcy."

"Interesting. I have never cared for that dance." The violinists began to scrape their bows across the strings of their instruments to tune them, requiring I speak a little louder. "You are kind to attend to Miss Elizabeth, but surely your partner is looking for you?"

I turned from her and helped Miss Elizabeth sit, which gave Bingley's sister little choice but to flounce away in high color.

Mrs. Bennet instantly filled the void left by Miss Bingley. "Lizzy, where is Jane? I do not yet know who will lead her out for the supper set." Her voice trembled with high drama. "I do not want her to throw away that dance on the likes of John Lucas."

"She is poised to begin the cotillion, Mama. You will have to wait to speak to her."

Mrs. Bennet let out a huff of impatience before she bustled toward the seats at the head of the dance where the matrons were perched like crows on a fence. Miss Elizabeth looked upon me with theatrical innocence and opened her mouth to say something witty when we were again interrupted.

"Why, Charlotte, I am very happy to see you," Miss Elizabeth said.

"I would be happier to see you partnered for the dance, Eliza. Does your ankle cause you much pain?"

"My ankle is *perfectly* tolerable, Charlotte," she said, slanting an amused glance at me, "but I believe Mr. Collins may be looking for you."

"For me?"

"He means to dance with you if you are free. He cannot trample me tonight, you see, and has singled out your toes for his attentions."

She laughed but scanned the crowd, saw Mr. Collins, and went directly to stand in his way. We were alone at last.

"Lizzy," cried my partner's youngest sister from ten paces away, "Wickham did not come!"

I stiffened and stared at the set that was forming. "But Mr. Denny is here and ready to dance with you, Lydia. You had better not leave him standing alone. Is everyone partnered?"

"Yes," she called over her shoulder, "even Mary who is to dance with poor John."

After a moment of silence, Miss Elizabeth said, "I wonder who next will appear to speak to us, Mr. Darcy. We have yet to hear of how a ball is conducted at St. James's or give Mr. Hurst directions to the refreshments."

I would have cast out a rejoinder were I not willing my heartbeat to return to a normal cadence. The mere mention of George Wickham would always cause my body to arm itself for war.

The magic had gone out of the evening for me. I floundered and could think of nothing innocuous to say. Meanwhile, Miss Elizabeth gave me a thoroughly intrusive examination with her perceptive eyes before settling back to watch the dancers.

Eventually, I cleared my throat and hoped that inspiration would come, but I was at a loss.

Finally, she took up the challenge. "I believe we must have *some* conversation, else I shall drift off to sleep where I sit."

"Very well. Do you read?"

"Indeed, I do!" she replied brightly. "I have even learnt my ABCs!"

My reply, which should have been to laugh, was stiff. "I did not mean to insult you. I only inquired as a means to spark a conversation. *I* for example, am reading a work by John Ritter on the confluence of ethical and scientific inquiry."

Both her eyebrows rose at once. "If you are determined to pursue that topic, you had best fetch me a pillow. My eyelids are becoming quite heavy just now, but my sister Mary would be delighted to hear your observations on Mr. Ritter."

Perhaps because I was discomposed by the mention of Wickham, or perhaps because I was suddenly aware of my deficiencies in the art of casual flirtation, her words stung me.

"Very well," I replied sharply, "tell me what I am to say, and I shall say it."

Elizabeth's Story...

I took in a breath, surprised—dismayed—by the biting tone of Mr. Darcy's challenge. We were settled next to a fern and far enough away from the musicians at the top of the room to speak conversationally, and if I could not dance, I had sincerely hoped for another round of his challenging repartee. What I was treated to, however, was the attention of a mostly mute and glowering statue who, when roused, decided we should speak of Ritter! When I balked at that, he barked at me.

"Tell me what I am to say, and I shall say it." Mr. Darcy's mouth was tight and obstinate as he spoke, rendering him irresistible to my provoking nature.

"Oh, if you leave it to me—"

"I do."

"Well then, let us get down to essentials, shall we? I have been trying to puzzle you out, and I find I am not getting on at all. Are you a harsh man?"

He uncrossed his arms and turned to look at me. "I certainly hope I am not."

"But you can be harsh in your opinions."

He frowned ever so slightly. "*You*, I believe, are an excellent judge of harsh opinions."

I smiled. How I love to be tested! "True, true," I mused, "but if you were to ask me whether I am a harsh woman, I would have to own it directly you see."

He looked uncomfortable and replied in irritable distraction. "To what end is this questioning, may I ask?"

"Well, if you insist upon bluntness, which I believe to be your preferred *mode,* then I shall lay out this before you: I have heard, from someone who claims acquaintance with you, that you are a harsh and unyielding man."

He paused. "Ah," he said flatly.

"That is your defense of yourself, sir? Ah?"

"What would you have me say? Naturally, I am harsh and unyielding when the circumstances demand I be so."

Mr. Darcy, standing beside me, struck me anew as a powerful, consequential man. Having grown up with Papa, who was snide rather than assertive, and Sir William Lucas, who confused congeniality with manliness, I momentarily lost the thread of my argument.

Faced with this force beside me, I fell to wondering whether perhaps I was out of my depth, and I would have retreated into lighter, jesting observations, but Mr. Darcy decided to coldly pursue my inquiry.

"Of what has George Wickham accused me, madam?"

"Of withholding a valuable living your father intended for him."

He snorted. "That old saw again?"

"Is it true? Will you not exonerate yourself?"

"I shall *not* lower myself to address that man's claims." He spat the words between clenched teeth.

I gasped in frustration. "Then he will be believed! Indeed, half the neighborhood is already sympathetic to him."

"And why should I care what this neighborhood thinks of me?"

This, of all the things he had said to me, struck me as unforgivably harsh. "Forgive me, sir," I said coldly. "I was mistaken in thinking that at least *my* opinion of you mattered."

Oh, for two good ankles! I would have walked away from him if I could. I looked around, desperate for someone to rescue me and caught Charlotte's eye. She came to me and, bless her, Mr. Darcy moved a few steps away so she could take up his place beside me.

Mr. Darcy's Story...

I AM NOT A CONVERSATIONALIST. I AM NOT INCLINED TO CHATTER amiably. That said, however, I had never massacred a conversation in the shocking manner in which I had just affronted Elizabeth Bennet. The task of reparation, of pulling together some semblance of conviviality between us, and of making an apology loomed before me. Having been toadied all my life, however, I was woefully unpracticed at groveling.

For a full minute, I stood beside Miss Elizabeth like an imbecile while my body reacted as though I had been struck a hard blow. As my wits began to thaw, I struggled for a strategy, and as though grasping at a straw, I decided to start by telling her about Wickham. Yes, that, I decided with relief, would be how I would begin. Of course, I would not mention Georgiana, but there was a great deal I could say.

I opened my mouth to begin anew, and I would have were it not for the abrupt arrival of Sir William's eldest daughter to entertain Miss Elizabeth. I moved away, as a gentleman should, and awaited my turn. But I did not move too far because I was determined to have a chance to defend myself. Eavesdropping is below me and I loathe it, but while lurking about by a sad-looking potted palm, I could not help but hear what was said.

"Did you enjoy your set, Charlotte?"

"Oh, well," the lady sighed. "I *was* glad to be led out for the opening dance, Eliza. John does not always remember that he has a sister who is not in the first tier of eligible girls."

"He was, however, kind enough to think of my sister Mary who is often left with the matrons."

Miss Lucas struck a resolute tone that prefaced a change of topic. "Eliza, do you really have no ambitions with regard to Mr. Collins?"

"My only ambition for my cousin is to be spared the mortification of refusing him should he resolve to pay his addresses. Why do you ask?"

"I would like to put myself forward. If you will not have him, and you say you will not, I would like to make myself an agreeable alternative."

After a heavy pause, Miss Elizabeth replied in disbelief. "Surely not, Charlotte."

"Why not? *You* have objections to him that you make plain to anybody, but I have no objections whatsoever."

"But think—what sort of life would you have? He has a strong inclination to dominate a woman with less power than he possesses, and yet he is thoroughly dominated by his patroness. I can think of no worse place to be situated! Below the salt to be sure. You would be little more than a drudge."

Then it was Miss Lucas's turn to pause. "You can think of no worse place, Eliza, because you are young yet. You are a very pretty girl with a lively air about you. In short, you have charm. You have prospects."

"I have no such thing. I fully expect to sit on the shelf, for I shall never marry without affection, without respect. And who comes to Hertfordshire? No one!"

"You have made my point for me. I, too, expect to sit on the shelf; yet, unlike you, I find the prospect unbearable. You will allow me to be unromantic if you are my friend, and you must understand that there is a great deal I would suffer to be mistress of my own home."

"Oh, Charlotte," Miss Elizabeth said softly.

"Do not pity me, Eliza. My eyes are open, and I know what I want. The only thing lacking is—"

"If you want my blessing, of course you have it, but I shall not lie and tell you how happy you make me with such a compromise."

They were silent for a moment, and then Miss Lucas said, "I shall be happy if I am lucky enough to secure your cousin."

Miss Elizabeth sounded slightly defeated when she eventually replied. "He will be lucky to get you. And if you are made mistress of Longbourn—"

"You will be family, and I shall not turn my back on you."

"I am not thinking of myself. Will you promise to take care of Mama? That is an enormous vow, I grant you, but if you will do it, then I shall be at peace with your choice."

"And you? Your sisters?"

"Jane cannot go to waste. If anything, my Uncle Gardiner will see her well settled with a good husband. My two youngest sisters are shaping up to be camp followers, and Mary will make someone a very tiresome governess."

"You may joke all you like. But what of you?"

"I shall find a caravan of gypsies and tell fortunes over a glass globe."

"I despair of you, my friend."

"I despair of myself. But would you be a dear and find my father? I wish to speak to him."

As Miss Lucas left, I pushed myself away from the wall only to have to step back to make way for Miss Bennet. I was finding my flirt's popularity quite tiresome and hoped for a reprieve from these eternal interruptions.

"Jane, dearest," Miss Elizabeth said with obvious affection, "do not let Mama see you standing idle. Is there not one marriageable man in the room with whom you have not danced?"

"How is your ankle, Lizzy?"

Miss Elizabeth did not care to be pitied. She ignored her sister's question and launched a question of her own. "Who has secured you for the supper set?"

Miss Bennet paused. "Mr. Bingley will take me in to supper."

"Will he? Mama will be in alt."

"Oh, Lizzy, do not tease me," Miss Bennet said in a low, pleading voice.

"But what is it? Surely you are pleased." Another pause. "Never tell me you have let Mr. Bingley crawl over your defenses."

"He has done so against my will."

"Then he has shown himself to be determined to earn your affection, and I applaud his resolve."

Miss Bennet's voice wavered. "I am torn in two."

"But why? If he loves you and you are inclined toward him, then why should he not offer for you?"

"Please God that he does not, Lizzy, because to refuse him will be unspeakably painful." She uttered this last on a stifled sob.

"You would refuse him?"

"I believe I must. He is everything good and amiable, a man perfectly suited to my temperament, and someone who has never discomposed me in any way. I could so easily love him. But his sisters are spiteful to Mama, and they cannot tolerate my own sisters. Could I be happy living with anyone who thinks ill of those dear to me?"

"Come, Jane. Surely you can see that those women will not always be living with their brother."

"The Hursts seem to be content to live with him. From what I gather, they follow him everywhere. And Miss Bingley, though she is elegant and has a fortune, is already six and twenty. This does not indicate to me she is much courted." Miss Bennet paused. "Even were she to marry and go away, there will always be society between us, and she will never let me forget her disapproval of my relations in trade."

"Though her own fortune comes from trade."

"How I wish they had never come here," Miss Bennet said sadly. "Oh, I must go. Mr. Parnell is coming to lead me out."

I looked out into the room and saw a homely man of middle years approaching. Behind him came Mr. Bennet, and I knew my moment still had not come.

"Did you indeed summon me, child?"

"Papa, how would you like to finish your evening with a book while I sit on a stool and toast us some cheese by the hearth?"

"Never tell me I am to be released from gaol!"

"You are. Will you call for the carriage? Harry can return for Mama and the others. My ankle is uncomfortable, and I would like to go."

Mr. Bennet tapped a footman on the shoulder and then came and took his daughter away. And thus ended my flirtation. Greatly sobered after such a disappointing evening, I realized what I must do, and on the following day, I did it.

Chapter 6

I was sunk in a kind of melancholy upon limping home from the ball at Netherfield. I had been forced to sit when I would rather dance and be gay, and I had been subjected to three horrible conversations. Charlotte would throw herself away on my cousin Collins. Jane had feelings for a man with spiteful sisters. It was discouraging news, indeed, and was preceded by Mr. Darcy uttering a sentence of such arrogance, such unholy self-consequence, that I could no longer like him.

But I did. I *did* like him! I liked the portion of him that engaged me, took charge of a situation, put me up on a horse, and made Mr. Collins go away.

Yet, I deplored the man I saw last night—the man too proud to justify himself to anyone. Instinct told me Mr. Wickham's charm was too lavish to believe. He used his gifts to his advantage, whereas Mr. Darcy had no charm at all and would never stoop to the use of an advantage even if it exonerated him from public disdain.

Mr. Darcy had disappointed me, and for that, I felt disinclined ever to forgive him. Jane was right. I, too, wished the Netherfield party had never come to Hertfordshire.

Only after recounting everything said to me fifty times over in my mind as I tossed and turned that night did I finally succumb to a fitful sleep. Feeling weary, sore, and vulnerable, I limped down to breakfast where I learned from my giggling sister Lydia that Mr. Collins asked Mama to speak to me alone. Could the day grow any worse? I sat still as a hare while my cousin stood before me and raised a finger as though he were addressing a congregation.

"Mr. Collins," I said, interrupting him before he began, "last night my friend Charlotte Lucas expressed such admiration for you! I begin to think that you would do well to court her, sir, for a more estimable and religious young lady I have never known."

My cousin stood before me with his finger still in the air, but now his jaw hung open, and so, speaking in a strong voice, I pressed on.

"I know you came here with the most generous intent of offering for one of us and thereby negating the sting of the entail. But upon knowing us better, you perceive that none of us would suit the life you so graciously offer—none, save Jane, of course, whom my mother reserves for Mr. Bingley."

He made a gurgle of protest, and I continued speaking on top of him. "I know you perceive that we are none of us made for religious life because a man of your intelligence cannot but see clearly. I am too headstrong to be agreeable to you. You were quite put out with me this week! I cannot change what I am, sir, and Mary cannot be livelier, Kitty more sensible, or Lydia made to behave with propriety."

Barely stopping for breath, I plowed ahead. "I am glad you sought me out this morning so I could advise you. Charlotte Lucas is a woman of character, modesty, and sense. You danced with her last night, and you must agree that Lady Catherine de Bourgh would be delighted to have someone like her at her parsonage." I stood abruptly and hobbled toward the door. "Miss Lucas has asked me to extend her invitation for dinner at Lucas Lodge. I believe she is very much in love with you!"

I left my cousin thunderstruck and went to my room where I penned a hasty note to Charlotte to expect Mr. Collins for dinner. Then I went to my mother who sat at her dressing table, humming and fluttering her handkerchief.

"Well, Lizzy?" Her eyes danced with delight. "What had Mr. Collins to say to you, hmm?"

"He told me I should leave Mr. Darcy alone."

"What?"

"Mr. Darcy stood beside me last night for a considerable time, and our cousin only wished to put me on my guard."

My mother huffed and sputtered. After a moment, she decided to be irate. "How dare he warn you off a gentleman of fortune who chooses to stand by you? No wonder he wished to be private. Had he said something of that nature with *me* in the room, I would have boxed his ears!"

"I believe he will dine with Sir William and Lady Lucas tonight, ma'am."

"Good riddance! I had hoped he would offer for you and—oh!" she wailed. "Hand me the vinaigrette."

"You are disappointed," I said after giving her the little glass vial, which she sniffed, "but Aunt Philips is having a card party to talk of last night with all the ladies of the neighborhood. Will you not go and hear what is being said of Jane? They will all tell you she was the most beautiful girl in the room."

She sat up. "Yes! Yes, I shall go. Get the girls to come too, will you, Lizzy?"

And thus, the morning was spent with my mother glowering at Mr. Collins as she bustled about, readying herself and her daughters for an afternoon at cards. My cousin, oblivious to the snubs of his hostess, went off in a daze to the home of a woman who was reportedly in love with him. My father retreated to his book room, and I went to sit in a patch of sunlight in the parlor with my foot on a stool.

I did not read, for I was not inclined to do so. I fussed the fringe on my shawl and thought of Charlotte and Jane and the dark truth of being a woman. We have no power. We have no safety to call our own unless we are independently wealthy and living in seclusion. We are kept like objects, and we must be careful—exceedingly careful—to find a man who treats his possessions well.

My mood darkened, my posture slouched, and the edges of my shawl turned into tangles. Then who should happen to appear abruptly in the doorway to see me this way but Mr. Darcy!

"Forgive me," he said stiffly. "The door was ajar, and I saw no one about."

"Mr. Darcy!" I gasped sitting upright.

"Pray do not stand, Miss Elizabeth. Is your father at home? I came only to have a word with him."

Thankfully, Mrs. Hill arrived a little breathlessly, and I asked her to announce Mr. Darcy to my father—and for goodness sake to close the front door left wide open by my younger sisters, no doubt. For the life of me, I could not think what to do. Part of me wished to go to my room so I would not have to see or speak to that man when he left. Another part wished desperately to know what he was saying to Papa.

Curiosity won the contest, aided by the discomfort of my ankle, and after a quarter of an hour, Mr. Darcy stopped at the doorway to the parlor and tipped his hat at me before gravely going down the hall, out the front door, and onto his horse.

PAPA HAD SHOWN MR. DARCY OUT, AS HE SHOULD, AND AFTER SEEING the man to the door, he came to stand in the parlor.

"Well, Lizzy?"

"What did Mr. Darcy say to you?"

"Oh, he came to be civil. He took his leave. Mr. Bingley goes to London on some trifling business, and Mr. Darcy returns to collect his sister and travel with her to their country estate."

My father, I could see, was being coy and trying to make me plead and cajole information from him. This was a game at which he was masterful. The more we tried to make him tell us a thing, the less inclined he was to do it because he enjoyed vexing us very much.

Swallowing my curiosity, I said, "I have to tell you something, Papa."

"Oh?" he replied with a sparkle in his eye.

I sensed he was hoping I would reveal something with regards to Mr. Darcy; instead, I said, "I am afraid I have played a trick on Mama."

He looked surprised. "Have you? What have you done?"

"I have sent Mr. Collins to pay court to Charlotte Lucas."

"You mean our cousin did not propose to you this morning?" my father asked with a puzzled frown. "He told me he would speak to you."

This irked me. Had my father been a better guardian, he would have discouraged his cousin out of consideration for me.

"I believe he planned to do so, but I interrupted him and told him Charlotte is in love with him. Which she is not, of course, but she told me last night that she would have Mr. Collins if she could get him."

"Well, well," he said, deflated.

"You are not put out, surely!"

"I am disappointed. I had a handy rejoinder prepared for your mother when you refused to marry the man and she insisted I make you change your mind." He paused. "Would you like to hear it?"

"No! No, I do not want to hear it! Are we all just a game to you? Have you no feelings? You wished to subject me to an uncomfortable proposal so you could be clever?" I was suddenly as angry as I had ever been with my father, and when he made some conciliatory noise, I savaged him.

"If you had only put as much effort into shaping and supporting your daughters as you have in harassing us with your wit, how much richer our lives would be, sir."

He shrugged, though I could see he was smarting. "I am an indolent parent."

"Indeed," I said gravely. "And look where it has gotten us. Lydia will throw herself at an officer and find herself ruined by the time she turns sixteen, and Kitty will harden into a fretful idiot. *Nothing* has gone into the education of my younger sisters, and only Mary feels the lack of it. She tries to fill herself with philosophy at least, though she is headed in a direction that will make her—has already made her—a pariah to people of sense. And Jane, who is a pearl, could easily attract a man of Mr. Bingley's worth. Indeed, she *has* attracted him, but that will all come to naught."

"Mr. Bingley seems to be making his way with our Jane in spite of us," my father said, his old irony returning.

"That is so, but Jane will refuse him if he comes to the point."

This remark got my father's attention. "Refuse him?" He shook his head. "No, no, Lizzy. There you are wrong, my girl."

"I am not wrong. She has told me as much. Mr. Bingley's sisters find us deplorable. We disgust them! Jane says she cannot marry into a family who despises those she loves." I took a breath and concluded my scolding. "Do not dare make a joke of *that*, sir. My sister is torn in two because you are an indifferent father."

Mr. Darcy's Story...

I SAT OPPOSITE BINGLEY AS MY COACH MADE FOR LONDON. MY MOOD was somber, as is common when one is forced to consequences they would rather not suffer. The legs of my pride had been cut off at the knees, I suppose, for I went as a cripple to Longbourn, the home of my conqueror. Miss Elizabeth looked young to me when I saw her on the sofa with her foot on a stool. She wore her hair in a simple style that made her face more beautiful somehow, and I wished—well, I could not allow myself to think of wishes, and I went to Mr. Bennet instead.

He greeted me with surprise, and I spoke without embellishment. George Wickham, I told him, was a known seducer, a gambler, and a cheat. Sketching an outline of my deep knowledge of the man I had known since childhood, I skirted around the incident of Ramsgate and said only that he had nearly ruined a young lady known to me. With cold precision I detailed the matter of the living at Kympton, the three thousand pounds George had since squandered, and the dates and amounts I settled with his creditors on four different occasions.

Mr. Bennet digested this news with reluctance. He did not strike me as a man who liked to be given something to do, and I had just tasked him with information to which he must necessarily attend.

"And why do you bring this to me, Mr. Darcy?" he asked in sour complaint, removing his spectacles and rubbing his eyes.

"Because your second daughter mentioned to me that Mr. Wickham claims to be the injured party, and he is believed in this society. He is a dangerous man, sir. There is little he will not do for money."

"What harm can he do here? None of us have fathered heiresses to tempt him."

"But if one of your daughters were abducted, you would pay a ransom, would you not?" This shocked Mr. Bennet, and he sat up. "George Wickham," I said plainly, "is a desperate man. I have rescued him for the last time. He has heavy debts in town, and his creditors will catch up to him. He is casting his net in this society, sir, to find a way out of difficulty."

"Why have you just now brought this forward?"

"I have been hesitant to speak because I wished to protect the good name of the young lady of my acquaintance. Wickham would not scruple to spread scandal if he were cornered. But I have begun to see that I must take the risk or else more harm will be done. You may do what you will with this information, sir," I said coldly. "I cannot stay and see things righted. I am needed at my estate, and I shall take my sister out of London for the winter."

What a dreadful task that had been! I had felt forced to confession, and it came out in a resentful burst, bitter and disgusted. But, having done the hard duty, relief came. Even if Wickham were to besmirch my sister's name in Hertfordshire, his career would come to an end now. I would give information to his creditors of his whereabouts and take Georgiana to the country, and we would survive the consequences no matter what came.

"You are never jolly," Bingley said, startling me out of my sober recollections, "but you are positively grave this morning."

I looked across the carriage at my friend. He had an expression of passive amiability on his face, which was his particular gift, and I wondered whether I should tell him what I had overheard. Yet, when I imagined telling him that Miss Bennet would refuse him should he offer and that his sisters' venom was principally to blame, I balked. Disclosures of this kind were anathema to me, and I had just been through the worst one of my life. For now, I decided I would stay out of Bingley's business.

But that same business would intrude. Two days later, he came to my townhouse.

London

"YOU WILL NEVER GUESS, DARCY! HURST HAS BROUGHT LOUISA AND Caroline back from Netherfield. They shut up the house and made it dashed difficult for me to return as I planned." He sighed loudly, which was the extent of his ability to express ire. "I wish they had not come. I would like to go back. There are—well, I enjoyed the country."

"Your sisters are able to decide for you then?" I asked in a sleepy, disinterested voice.

"Well, you know Caroline. She is impossible when she does not get her way."

And so, I offered one observation. "I pity the girl you marry if your sister is to be mistress of you in perpetuity."

He looked startled. "But she will not always be with me. Caroline *will* marry."

"She has yet to do so, my friend, though she is elegant and rich.

Does that not tell you something?"

He looked puzzled because he was not an analytical fellow. At last, his brow cleared, and he laughed. "But she is waiting for you to make her an offer!"

"She will never have me. You must tell her to move on from that ambition."

He sighed once again, and so I asked him about his business. Bingley has a hundred thousand pounds in trust as his fortune, but he has a few remaining factories that he has been slowly selling off to distance himself altogether from the taint of trade. His sojourn to town was for the purpose of disposing of a china factory. Once we had dispensed with that topic, I told him I was taking Georgiana to Pemberley, and we parted ways with cordiality.

I wondered what would happen to my good-natured friend. He was faced with two paths: either he would be his own man or live a life dominated by his older sisters. Having filial shortcomings of my own to address in the months to come, I turned my attention away from Bingley and toward my sister.

Chapter 7

Life at home became tiresome. The Bingleys had decamped, taking Mr. Darcy and his provocations away as well as dampening any hope for an advantageous marriage for my sister. Mr. Collins's head was turned by Charlotte's unrelenting attentions, and my mother was furious.

One evening, she went so far as to bring up a testy subject that distressed me, for I had told her the lie that Mr. Collins warned me off Mr. Darcy, and I thought my moment of reckoning had come.

"Mr. Collins, I understand you remonstrated with my daughter Elizabeth with regard to her friendship with Mr. Darcy," my mother said in a voice of injured dignity.

How startled I was when Mr. Collins replied with a sanctimonious sniff!

"Indeed, madam. Mr. Darcy is to marry his cousin Anne, the daughter of Lady Catherine de Bourgh. I do not think it seemly that my cousin Elizabeth should cast out lures to a man already affianced."

A hot flush of dismay flooded my face, and I sat helplessly exposed in front of my family. First, my mother had said plainly that Mr. Darcy and I had been universally seen as friends, and then I learned that Mr. Darcy was spoken for. Only at that awful moment did I realize I had fostered some hope of a union in the dark recesses of my mind.

The man's pride, taciturn nature—his unvarnished sense of superiority notwithstanding—and even his *harshness* were unbearably attractive to me. These contrary traits coupled with his intelligence, his confidence in the world, his supreme independence, and his unapologetic male power had been irresistible. And yes, we had been friends in the making. I could easily see myself teasing and provoking him even in old age.

As though this moment of self-realization were not a form of crucifixion in itself, my father thought to add to my dismay.

"Of whom are we speaking?" he asked with an air of distraction that did not fool me.

"Of Mr. Darcy," Mama said. "He paid a great deal of attention to both our oldest girls. Lizzy, in particular, seemed to capture his interest."

"Ah yes, Mr. Darcy," he mused as though trying to recall the man. "Did I mention he came to see me?"

"To see you, Mr. Bennet? But what could he have to say?"

"He came to tell me that our daughters' favorite beau, Mr. Wickham, is a vicious character." My father spoke casually though he glanced at me with pointed interest.

My reaction was no less than that of anyone else in the room: we sat in shock.

Lydia cried out in protest. "Surely not, Papa!"

"I am afraid so. The least of his shortcomings of character is that he is pursued for debts unpaid. If the bailiffs catch him, which I expect to happen any day now, he will abscond from here on the run or be taken to Fleet Street."

"But that is because Mr. Darcy did not give him the living for which he was groomed!" howled Kitty.

"That tale was a fabrication. Mr. Darcy settled three thousand pounds in lieu of the living Mr. Wickham claimed he did not want. A tidy sum your favorite spent in dissipation, which led him to seek shelter in the militia."

"And the worst of his character, sir?" I asked coldly, for I knew the answer already. Such smoothness of address and such intimate knowledge of what is flattering to a woman spoke volumes to me.

"He is a danger to young ladies, and I hope, Mrs. Bennet, that you will never allow the lecher proximity to your daughters again."

"Well!" huffed Mama. "Well! He is a scoundrel you say? But his manners are so very engaging."

"A villain, my dear, has taken tea in your parlor a dozen times at least."

Lydia burst into noisy tears, Kitty put a handkerchief to her nose, and Mary looked poised to say she had known the man was evil all along. Mr. Collins meanwhile smirked at my family who had been blind to wickedness, and so I picked up my book and my candle and went to bed.

The next morning after breakfast I went to my father.

"Well, Lizzy, your Mr. Darcy is spoken for. Have you recovered from your heartbreak?"

I knew what tack to take with my father. "You know me very well, sir. I have a weakness for enraging men."

"I hope I am one such man."

"You are, but if you want an apology from me, I shall give it. I do not care to fight with you."

"I shall ask for no apology from you if you demand none from me."

"I did not come for that, sir. I came to ask whether you would do me a great service."

"I am inclined to hear you. I like a girl who has been crossed in love."

"Indeed, I am very happy to be in love with Mr. Darcy. I have no hope of winning him, you see, and so I can be comfortable as I pine away my youth. But in truth, Papa, I have no stomach to see my dearest friend being courted by our mortifying relative. And with Mr. Bingley gone and Netherfield closed, I am made miserable by Mama's fretting. Will you send me to London, sir?"

"You wish to be spared what the rest of us must endure?"

"My ankle pains me still," I said in deadly seriousness. "I cannot make my escape out of doors as I used to."

He frowned a little. "I shall ask your uncle to have a doctor see you."

"I would be very grateful, but that is not the only boon I ask."

His brow cleared, and he regarded me with a wry look. "I see I am not to apologize for the faults of my parenting, but I shall be made to pay regardless."

"I wish you would send Jane with me. Mama harasses her day and night to marry Mr. Bingley, as though my sister could conjure him on bended knee."

"Both sensible daughters are to go? A heavy penalty, Lizzy. Well, if you must go and take Jane, you must. But I shall not sit still for what is left. I believe your mother should have a holiday in Bath, at least until our cousin has married her rival's daughter. Mr. Collins can batten himself on Sir William," he said, sitting comfortably back in his chair with his hands folded over his belly, "and I shall have peace for once."

Chapter 8

Mr. Darcy's Story…

I left London on a cold, windy early December day. My sister and her companion sat in the forward-facing seat and I, on the rear-facing bench, was left to contemplate not only Georgiana's defeated little face, but the road behind me.

A flirtation begun with swords crossed out of irritation had proceeded along the lines of lightly erotic riposte and had abruptly culminated in a deadly contest. Miss Elizabeth had begun to believe she had power over me, so I had skirted directly beneath her guard and sliced through her vanity. She lunged out of instinct, piercing me to the bone. My confidence, my sense of consequence, still bled weeks later.

Just as Miss Elizabeth had watched me speak to Sir William Lucas, I watched myself as though through her eyes. Against my will, I observed the subtle and indelicate ways I asserted my superiority over everyone. Had I ever met anyone I felt to be my equal?

The answer startled and appalled me. When I ate a meal in a public room, my every movement was not only meant to feed myself but to show those watching the elegance and refinement of my upbringing.

When I spoke to an innkeeper, my tone demanded, expected, and threatened all at once. When we changed horses in Highgate, the greeting of a friendly curate elicited the barest nod. I stood in weary impatience as an innkeeper in Stamford attended a middling sort of gentleman. People were either useful or in the way, but they were never deserving of my notice.

One evening after we arrived at Pemberley and sat down to supper, I asked, "Georgiana, have I become arrogant do you think?"

Over the days since my return from Hertfordshire, I had tried to regain some of our former ease with one another. My sister proved a tough nut, but I was determined to spend the winter chipping away at her dejection. Having discovered that trying to draw Georgiana out of her turtle shell to confide in me was pointless, I had the dimly lit idea to bring her a little into my confidence.

Her eyes darted up from her plate. "What do you mean?"

"Have I become as insufferable as Lady Catherine?"

For a second, I thought she would reply in her usual mode, which was to blush and stammer and plead helpless ignorance of any topic I brought up. But we were alone. She had no one to run to, for her companion, Mrs. Annesley, was in bed with a headache.

"I-I do not know, William. I had not thought of it," she said, and I imagined another night would proceed without any progress being made between us.

But the clocks at Pemberley had a trick of ticking loudly and accentuating not only reverberating silence but, on certain very cold nights, uncanny isolation. After a moment of profound silence in that great house, Georgiana looked up from her plate again and spoke.

"Why do you ask?"

My heart soared. "I met a lady in Hertfordshire who laughed at me for my manners."

"She laughed at you?"

"You sound shocked. I suppose no one dares to laugh at me, which is answer enough to my question."

After a moment's hesitation, my sister spoke again. "Who was the lady in Hertfordshire?"

"Miss Elizabeth Bennet," I replied, surprised by the sound of conscious pleasure in my voice for having named her aloud.

We spoke no more about Miss Elizabeth that evening. But at dinner the following night, Georgiana shyly asked, "Were you very angry when Miss Elizabeth laughed at you?"

Now *my* eyes were the ones to dart up from my plate in surprise. "Do you know, I enjoyed being laughed at a little." And after a pause, I said, "But I have begun to wonder whether I should try, at least, to be more agreeable."

"To please the lady?"

"I doubt I shall ever see her again, but if I should, I hope she would be baffled by an altogether better impression of me."

Georgiana's brow creased into a tiny, puzzled frown. "Did you argue with her?"

"Regularly. Do not distress yourself. The lady—"

"Miss Elizabeth."

"Yes. She has a penchant for provoking me."

Chapter 9

With relief, Jane and I sought sanctuary at the home of Aunt and Uncle Gardiner. They lived in the city proper in Cheapside, close to Uncle's business. My aunt kept a lively and fashionable home, and she was young enough to share interests with my sister and me.

The day after our arrival, a doctor came to see me. I expected a round, gray-haired gentleman, and upon welcoming a tall, thin young man with a shock of red hair and lively blue eyes, I felt slightly discomposed to give myself over to his examination. My aunt stood in the room, and Jane sat on a chair beside me. I was propped up in bed on top of the counterpane, dressed but without shoes or stockings. My bare feet I hid under a shawl.

The *child*, as I thought of him despairingly, introduced himself as Mr. Bromley. He smiled and received Aunt Gardiner's kindest greeting along with her explanation of my injury and her concerns. Jane, too, seemed disposed to be charmed and smiled openly when Mr. Bromley looked at her. I, however, greeted him with barely concealed suspicion.

For one, he was too young to know anything; for another, I was disinclined to like doctoring of any kind.

Then came the moment for his examination, and before my eyes, the amiable young man sharpened into an intensely focused instrument of science. With a frown of concentration, he manipulated my good and then my painful ankle. He felt, poked, and pushed here and there and then looked me over head to toe and back again with the eye of a mathematician.

"This is a simple case of overuse, Mrs. Gardiner. Your niece"—he turned and included me in his conclusion—"does not appear to me to be a lady who sits idle. The joint cannot heal if it is put under repeated pressure. You will not like this, Miss Elizabeth, but I shall sentence you to two weeks at the very least of only the lightest use."

"I am to be bed bound, sir?" I asked irritably.

"You are to be bed bound for as many hours as you can tolerate. You may sit in a chair if you are meticulous in putting your ankle on a stool and never putting weight downward onto that foot." He now looked much older as he spoke to me in a firm voice of authority, and upon glancing at Jane, I saw that her eyes had drifted up to gaze at him.

"And the ankle will heal?" Aunt Gardiner asked.

"If Miss Elizabeth is scrupulous in resting it—yes." He turned back to me. "As I said, you appear a very active lady, and I can assure you that, if you take my advice, you will be just as active as you like after a few weeks. However, if you insist upon testing the joint or thinking that use before it heals will make it stronger, you will find yourself frequently in pain and susceptible to injury for a very long time if not the rest of your life."

That pronouncement frightened me, and I could think of nothing to say.

"Thank you, Mr. Bromley," Jane said to cover my silence. She rose and, with my aunt, saw the man out while I lay back with a sigh.

Two days later, I sat fretful and cross and wondered whether a person could go mad from inactivity. For some reason, my relatives decided I should be treated not only as a stationary object but a sick one. I was cosseted with trays in bed, oceans of quietude, and whispers of compassionate solicitude. Fearing I would soon scream aloud, I wrote to my father.

Dearest Papa,

I have seen a doctor, and I am chained to a bed! I must have help down the stairs, which I am allowed to do once a day, only to be hustled up them again after half an hour and tucked up with a posset. I have been a drain on your purse already, and I know sending Mama and my sisters to Bath was an expense, but if you can spare it, I ask for some funds with which to hire a music master. I mean to learn to play better if I can do nothing else, and my doctor has given his conditional approval after explaining how I may sit at the instrument. If lessons are not possible, then I shall endure, hopefully without committing violence on the next person to put their hand on my forehead.

My father's reply came with a note to Uncle Gardiner about the expense of a music master, and a week later, I sat at the pianoforte performing for my tutor. As I played, he listened gravely to ascertain my level of skill, and then we began to work in earnest. Having nothing better to do, I practiced diligently, and when he came for the second lesson, I had mastered what he asked me to do in the first. My progress pleased me, but the master, Mr. Finch, expressed only mild approval. However, over the next few weeks, he pushed me to take on more demanding pieces.

One day, after I had demonstrated my scales to warm up my hands, I decided to engage him in conversation.

"Do you have many pupils hereabouts, Mr. Finch?" I asked.

My music master was a small man with a sharp nose and overlarge ears. He looked to be forty years old, was neat as a pin, and regular as a clock. I began to like him very much, for he was predictable and possessed of a comfortable evenness of temper.

"Not many, Miss Elizabeth. At this time of year, some of my pupils go into the country. I made time for you because a young lady I have instructed for years went to Derbyshire."

A little bell rang in my mind. "I hear much of Derbyshire lately. Have you been there?"

"I have been fortunate to travel, yes. Last summer I was invited to Pemberley, an estate in that county, to work intensively with my pupil."

"Pemberley! You teach Miss Darcy, then?"

He looked startled and chagrined. "I make it a habit not to mention names. I have perhaps said too much."

"I have met Mr. Darcy, sir. I do not intend to gossip." But of course I wished he would fill my head with tittle-tattle about the Darcys. In consequence, I pressed very lightly for more from him on the subject. "Miss Darcy must be very accomplished?"

"She is indeed a proficient."

"I am sure she is. I have heard as much from Miss Bingley. Might you unbend just an inch, and tell me whether Pemberley is as grand as I am told?"

"I do not believe there is a more beautiful estate, miss."

"My word! Have you been to many such places then?"

He glanced at me with an expression of mild indulgence. "I do not care to say."

Ah well. I had to be content with this teaspoon of information, and setting Miss Darcy's proficiency as my ideal, I applied myself with renewed vigor to my studies. I had performed at Lucas Lodge in the presence of Mr. Darcy—a simple country tune I had well mastered that neither embarrassed me nor impressed anybody. There would never be an occasion for me to exhibit in front of the man again, but I could imagine his surprise—his comeuppance—to hear a middling country girl play with true finesse.

My efforts received mixed reviews, however. I knew I had gone wrong one evening when Jane, who sat knitting while I practiced, said, "Lizzy, to what end is this war with the pianoforte?"

"War?" I asked in surprise. Indeed, I had just conquered a Mozart piece and was feeling smug.

Jane is as mild tempered as a flower, but she can sometimes speak bluntly. "Your playing begins to remind me of Mrs. Hurst."

"Mrs. Hurst plays at a very high level," I replied with dignity.

"She does, I grant you, but there is an air of flaunting in her style, do you not agree?"

I frowned and opened my mouth to argue but could not defend against what my sister said. Jane was right! While the fingering, complexity, and lack of errors were all laudable in Mrs. Hurst's playing, her execution was in the order of a statement of superiority that was not pleasing to the humble ear.

At last, I said, "You are so right. I have been practicing as a form of revenge, and the result is—well, what is the result?"

"Your music is angry. I preferred your natural ease, your delight in a simple tune."

"Perhaps I can climb off my high horse and improve my playing without losing myself. I thank you for correcting me."

"But, with whom are you angry? What is the revenge you speak of?"

"I have been trying to clear the eyes of the Darcys and Bingleys of the world. Nonsensical, I know, for I doubt I shall ever have the chance to do so in reality. They made me feel inferior, or perhaps they made me wish to be superior."

I laughed at knowing myself better and tried the Mozart again in a sweeter state than I had begun.

Chapter 10

Mr. Darcy's Story...   *Pemberley*

Winter progressed as it always does in the country. The branches of the trees turned bare, the drizzles and sleeting rains came and went, and when the sun peeked out, the sky over all the gray world turned a shade of violet blue. Snow fell and melted while the work of the estate went on like the cogs of a clock.

Pemberley ran herself. We masters come and go, but the land breathes through its cycles, fallow followed by greening, unimpressed by our fiddling.

I kept occupied. There was still much to be done to make sure the estate continued to run tick tock year over year. When not pouring my attention into the management of my legacy, I made sure I was close to my sister so that she might feel easier with me and perhaps even acquit herself of guilt over Wickham.

Of that blackguard, I heard nothing. This signified to me that he had escaped with his skin somehow and that, for the nonce, my sister's reputation remained intact. All the same, I sent a note to my cousin Colonel Richard Fitzwilliam and tasked him with making inquiries as to the disposition of our nemesis. Then I went to find my sister.

The fence I had been avoiding had to be jumped sooner or later, and I chose to ride straight at it. Georgiana was a tall, slender girl, still sometimes awkward in her movements but beginning to exhibit those attributes society identifies as elegant. Her face was not beautiful, but her features were regular, and there was an openness in her countenance that was undeniably appealing. She was, to me, a striking woman in the making, if only she could find a particle of confidence.

I could never think of a confident woman without thinking of Elizabeth Bennet, and I wondered briefly how she had weathered the attentions of her ridiculous parson cousin. That the man must have smarted from a bloody refusal I did not doubt.

"What amuses you, William?" Georgiana asked. I must have smiled at these ruminations.

"Oh, nothing in particular. Will you sit down to play commerce?"

We had long ago, out of necessity, devised a way that just the two of us could play, and Mrs. Annesley, seeing us occupied, left us alone for the afternoon.

"Did I tell you I stumbled across George Wickham in Hertfordshire?" I began in the most casual voice I could conjure as I looked over my cards.

Her eyes widened, and I knew she was scouring my face with them. I kept my eyes on my cards and blithely spoke on. "He was making himself agreeable with the neighborhood, and so I informed against him with the money lenders."

She gasped and put her cards face down. I did not let her gather herself to speak, and still in an attitude of distraction over the arrangement of my hand, I said, "I believe he escaped, but I would imagine he is living in the rough now. I wrote to Richard to find out what he can. My best hope is the scapegrace is on a ship to New South Wales."

After a gulp, my sister asked in an unsteady whisper, "And did he speak—"

"Of you? No, I do not believe he did. We would have heard the tattle from our Matlock relations if he had." I put my cards down and looked at her. "There is a possibility he tried that ploy and was not believed, Georgiana. The word of a swindler, which is what he is at heart, is eventually disregarded. At any rate, Richard will find out what has become of Wickham, and we shall wash our hands of him, shall we?" I spoke lightly and with as much kind commiseration as I could interlace into a voice more accustomed to officious speaking.

"I-I cannot keep secret what I have done," she said in quiet misery. Her cards, too, lay on the table between us.

"You do not have to. The shame is not yours to hide—it is mine for not caring for you better and Wickham's for being a scoundrel."

"You have always cared for me," she said more forcefully.

"No, not always. I should have been more forthcoming. Over the years, I could have told you of my misgivings about Wickham's character, of his dissipation, and of his desperation for money. When he came sniffing around, you would have been made uneasy and suspicious."

"But would I, William? I-I have no confidence that I am not the stupidest gull."

That, I realized, was the most confident thing I had ever heard my sister say. I smiled at her, a fulsome grin of approval.

"You are a Darcy, love. We are *not* stupid. Proud and disagreeable perhaps, but never stupid. Do look at your cards, Georgiana. I have a decent hand that I do not want to waste."

That solid thud of landing safely—brilliantly—on the other side of a high wall filled my awareness. My sister seemed to feel it too, and we enjoyed the most pleasant game of cards we had ever played on that wet afternoon in January.

IN THE WEEKS THAT FOLLOWED, MY SISTER WARMED TO ME AND settled into a comfortable trust that I still held her in esteem. She also developed a curious and often unsettling fascination with Miss

Elizabeth Bennet. She asked one day whether I would describe her.

"Oh—well, she is hardly what I would call beautiful. Short. Dark-haired."

"Has she no redeeming features?" Georgiana asked in surprise.

"Oh, she has many. Her eyes are enchanting—very fine and dark but shining too. Hard to describe. And she moves like a dancer."

"What do you mean?"

"She has a natural grace and strength. She is a strong walker."

"Is she?"

I indulged this fascination. We had so little to talk about over the years because of our disparate ages and circumstances, so any topic that kept us speaking I would have blown upon as a faint ember in the hearth.

Never once did I stop to consider to what end my sister pressed for information about Elizabeth Bennet, but she showed her hand by asking, "Will you go back to Hertfordshire to court her then?"

We were bundled to our ears and walking to the lake to see whether there was enough ice for skating.

"Who? Elizabeth Bennet? No!" I protested. And then, thinking to disabuse her of this romantic notion, I said, "No, no. She is not eligible, you see."

"Not eligible? But why? Is she not a gentleman's daughter?"

"She is that. But she has relations in trade," I said with finality—that being the beginning and the end of all my objections.

"As do the Bingleys," Georgiana replied.

From the mouths of babes! My sister looked at me with curiosity, almost with a demand in her voice to have the matter explained in plain English.

"Well...um," I stammered. "But, Bingley also has a fortune, you see." She frowned a little, and I plowed on. "The Bennet family is, in the main, a haphazard bunch. The younger girls are ignorant and wild to a fault, Mrs. Bennet has the manners of a market seller, and

Mr. Bennet is a wit. Excepting Elizabeth and her older sister Jane, the Bennets are not relations of whom I could be proud." I ended this speech on a hard note.

My sister fell silent, and I breathed a sigh of relief that she had dropped her mad notion. A match with Elizabeth Bennet? Impossible!

Chapter 11

Over the course of December, my ankle healed, and my skill at the pianoforte deepened. By January, I felt equal to going home. My mother's holiday with Kitty, Lydia, and Mary had been a disappointment. Due to Papa's paltry notion of generosity, they stayed in mediocre lodgings, and therefore, they had been treated as every other country bumpkin who visited Bath to mingle with high society, which is to say that the best they managed was a public assembly during which none of my sisters was asked to dance.

My father wrote to me of this with a smirk of satisfaction between the lines, my sister Mary wrote of the trip with heavy disapprobation for being a waste of time, and Kitty wrote a petulant little note about how horrid Bath was and how she hoped never to go again. My sister Lydia did not write, but I heard in dribs and drabs from all three letters that she was in the sulks. The officers of the militia had gone away, and she was left with the country boys she had known all her life. Meanwhile, Charlotte married Mr. Collins, and my mother, who had hoped to come home from holiday with three husbands in tow, was in a fit of dejected self-pity.

"I must go home," I told Jane one night after Three Kings' Day.

Jane had bloomed in London. My aunt always had company at her table, and while we visited, she made sure she entertained as many young men as she could. Not only was Jane a favorite of the son of Uncle Gardiner's banker, who stood to inherit both a business and a fortune, but she was called upon with great regularity by a man who had risen in the ranks of the East India Company and a barrister whose father was a ranking member of the House. Mr. Charles Bingley's star faded in the dawn of her new popularity with men who liked her relations very well, or so it seemed to me. But it was the lowly young doctor with boyish freckles that kept Jane in high sparkle.

Mr. Bromley came to look at me once a week, and my aunt Gardiner kept him for tea if she could. She looked wisely from my sister to the young man and asked him to look into the throats of her children. This gave him the handy excuse to come twice a week, and when my nephew bent his thumb backward in a violent scuffle with his sister in the nursery, he came more often still.

My uncle Gardiner, upon seeing this man always in his house, took pains to be home from his warehouse for tea and invited Mr. Bromley to a lecture one night and a dinner with his contemporaries the next. I wondered whether he was sounding out the doctor with regards to his means and intentions, and I was soon enlightened when he brought up the subject over dinner.

I have often pondered the strange dichotomy between my mother, who is silly and uneducated, and her brother, my uncle, who is a man of both sense and consideration. This difference between siblings was never clearer than when Uncle Gardiner began to tell us at dinner of Mr. Bromley's family and circumstances.

Whereas my mother would have spouted wild, suggestive nonsense, from my uncle we heard rational facts. The young man was not wealthy, but he had a decent competence from a landed uncle. His own father, now living in leisure in Berkshire, had also been a doctor, so he was the son of a gentleman at least. Young Mr. Bromley's status dwelt in that strange state that hung between gentleman and yeoman. He could marry credibly either up or down but would add no consequence to a lady or provide for her other than passably.

These facts were delivered in a way that spared us all consciousness and embarrassment. My sister was not studied to see how this news fell on her. She was gently and with great consideration told Mr. Bromley's status without any intent to either encourage or dissuade her. The decision, my uncle made clear, was hers to make. For this great discretion, I admired Uncle Gardiner more than ever and thought despairingly of Mr. Darcy who would never know what an exceptional *tradesman* I had as a relation.

Jane seemed inclined to take her time with her suitors, and while I was anxious to go home and pull my family's spirits up from the doldrums, she hesitated. In the end, we decided Jane should stay, ostensibly to help my aunt with her children who were on the verge of *catching colds* all winter, and I would go to Longbourn.

RETURNING HOME WAS WORSE THAN I THOUGHT IT WOULD BE. Confined in a house with no new or exciting visitors, my sisters were forever cross with one another. My father looked weary, and my mother looked older, and both were somehow more disagreeable than ever. I did what I could for Mama by telling her in minute detail about Jane's many admirers. Lydia and Kitty were drawn into these conferences out of boredom and romantic leanings. They began to speak better to one another and to talk of the number of beaus they would attract when their turns came to go to Aunt Gardiner's house. My mother's thoughts slowly turned away from her defeats, and she once again went out visiting in the neighborhood to gossip about Jane's conquests.

For Papa, I could do nothing. He was disinclined to be cheered, so I turned my attention to my middle sister, Mary.

"I had a music master in London while my ankle healed," I told her one day.

"Yes, I heard," she said without pulling her nose out of her book.

"He taught me a very great deal. Would you like me to show you a little of what I learned?"

She puckered up with pride. We Bennets were testy that way, but she acquiesced with a gloomy shrug; by week's end, we had established a habit of practicing together. At first, Mary did not like my corrections. She had always been the better player even though she lacked style. But my improvements had rendered me, in comparison to her, an expert, and she gradually paid more attention to what I had to share. Without Jane, I grew closer to Mary, and by February, she had become a softer version of herself.

Not only had I helped Mary with her playing, I also cut my sister's hair and put it in a more flattering style, and when we visited friends, I brought her forward and included her in conversation. I somehow convinced her that looking into the mythology of the Greeks would complement her Christian education, and we read of Mythos and Pathos, of the kings of Ithaca and Athens, and of Poseidon and Apollo. I sat patiently as I listened to her assessments of their moral failures and lightly pointed out the lessons we could take away from these tales in a more practical, less critical light.

The lesson I learned was this: attention will do what lectures will not, and while my youngest sisters remained giddy and empty-headed, my middle sister I salvaged from the dung heap. Let Miss Bingley and Mrs. Hurst see us now, and they would have to amend their impression to say the *three* eldest Bennet girls, at least, were presentable.

That I continued to let the opinions of our elegant visitors of last fall goad me in my private thoughts was a nuisance I could not seem to conquer. When I went anywhere, I strove to be on my best behavior as though in answer to their criticisms all those months ago. I cannot be other than myself, but the edge of my impertinence had ground away, and being always with my staid sister lent me a little steadiness, a bit of dignity.

March came with rain and news that Jane would marry Mr. Bromley. Mama did not know whether to be in alt or crushed.

"But why did she not pick the young man with the fortune?" she mourned in one breath, and in the next, "But married! Jane will be Mrs. Bromley and live in London. I am sure her husband will be a famous town doctor, a *gentleman* doctor, who will only see members of Parliament and important figures at court."

"You may believe that if it pleases you," my father said glumly.

Mr. Bromley was due to visit Friday with settlements after earning my uncle's provisional approval and having secured my father's written consent. Papa did not like to put himself to the trouble of securing Jane's happiness, it seemed, or he felt himself to be judged against my uncle's successful efforts to secure my sister a respectable future. Either way, he was cantankerous throughout the visit.

Mr. Bromley began to impress me, however. My father's incivility did not daunt him in the least. Nor did my mother's mortifying compensation for Papa's manners. Mama's enthusiasm, her effusions over him, and our raucous dinnertime ritual at Longbourn amused him, and he even participated by telling a few jokes. Seeking to salvage something of decorum, Mary and I performed a few duets after dinner before the poor man was compelled to play cards with Mama, Kitty, and Lydia. My father wandered away with his candle, and I writhed inwardly at the very thought of passing such an evening with Mr. Darcy instead of our easily pleased Mr. Bromley.

Thankfully, the following day brought Jane home. She came with the Gardiners and their children, and the sheer number of people present already known to my sister's intended distanced him from our awkward manners. Aunt Gardiner and her children filled the room and surrounded him with easy recollections of visits and common acquaintances. He examined a scrape on little Eddie's elbow with professional gravity and felt little June's neck for lumps, declaring her safe from putrid throat. And Uncle Gardiner did his part too by pulling him into intelligent conversation or inviting him to ride when the weather permitted.

Uncomfortable as I was, Jane looked upon the whole with steadiness and complacency that surprised me.

"You are happy, Jane," I said one evening, almost betraying the surprise this realization caused me. Mary sat on my bed reading with a shawl over her legs, and Jane brushed out my hair.

"I am. There is substance in him, Lizzy."

"You do not need to justify your choice to me. He cured my ankle, and for that he is due any prize, even my sister." I chuckled.

"What sort of life will you have?" Mary asked.

Jane looked at our sister in the mirror with an expression of surprise. She was unused to having Mary in the room with us and forgot we were not alone.

"I shall have a useful life," she said after a thoughtful pause. "I shall run a house and perhaps have more duties than I am used to."

"Will you?" I asked.

"I shall learn to cook a little, I hope. At the very least, I am determined to become proficient at jam," she said, and I feared I would burst out laughing. "I have always wanted to do so, but Mama has insisted we are above the kitchen. Of course, I shall sew and manage the accounts, and I shall also see his visitors. I believe there are people who come every day to be seen."

"Your house will be *open* then?" Mary asked in surprise.

"Yes. Robert spends the mornings in his consulting rooms at his home and the afternoons visiting the bed bound."

"Will you go dancing?" I asked in a fair imitation of my sister Lydia.

Jane smiled, and I saw in her expression that she was content. "Not often, Lizzy. Mr. Bromley goes out at all hours if needs must. I shall wait up for him and keep the teapot ready. You may laugh at me, but that is a life that thrills me to think on it. How much more comfortable I shall be to be useful than to be on the arm of a rich man, going to balls and parties! No, I am a homebody and only want to care for someone who is useful in the world."

"That is precisely what I hope for," Mary said quietly.

Suddenly, what *I* wished for in life loomed large. I wished to be mistress of a large estate, married to a rich and arrogant man whom I teased relentlessly into a more joyful state. Certainly, I wished to make myself useful in a great house and to the people who served it. But I also wished to hear great music, to see great art, to visit great cities, and to participate in great conversation. I wished to be educated and *worldly*! I wanted very good clothes and the best of everything. I also wanted the freedom to walk the lanes of a beautiful property as though it were my own without a care in the world. Perhaps in the company of a man who compliments, rather than condemns, my strong walking. Good lord! Mary would hardly countenance these unspiritual aspirations, and Jane would look at me with despairing pity for aiming impossibly high.

THE DAYS PASSED WITH ENDLESS TUMULT. THE GARDINERS LEFT WITH Mr. Bromley, and Mama set about preparing for a wedding that was months away with all the serenity of a Bedlamite in mental crisis. The weather was grizzly, and I rarely had the opportunity to run away. Nor could I escape into music. Mary and I were deemed too noisy when we played. We interfered with important business and were shooed out of the way.

Jane was never free, leaving the only respite to be our room where I retreated regularly. Alone, I could not help but think with a tinge of horror upon the future I envisioned as my ideal—the impossible future upon which I had stupidly fixed my hopes. To be the helpmate of a vicar, the wife of a councilman seeking a seat in town government, or the missus of some gentleman's dull, little house all struck me as worse than spinsterhood. A mediocre future did not appeal, and yet such was my destiny—if I were lucky! Hopeless!

Thankfully, my good friend Charlotte rescued me from Longbourn and the unhappy turn of my reflections. She wrote and asked whether I would visit when her sister Maria and Sir William came at Easter. It was with astonishing haste that I agreed to go. Jane would not be married until June, and I thought I might go mad in the interim. Even the prospect of visiting the home of my prosy Cousin Collins did not dampen my enthusiasm, and my father, bearing no expense at all, only shrugged and waved me away, telling me to do as I pleased.

I replied eagerly, accepting Charlotte's invitation, and having nothing else to do, wrote a long letter about our family doings. After chronicling the minutiae of Jane's betrothal, I wrote of Mary's improvement and my efforts there in some detail. Of my younger sisters, I said only that they were much as they always were. This resulted in an immediate reply asking whether Mary would also like to visit. Charlotte reassured me that Mr. Collins approved of my middle sister, and upon having read my letter, he thought to invite her. Mary expressed a reserved sort of acquiescence, but I knew she, too, was wild to go, and off we went to see Kent for the first time.

Chapter 12

Mr. Darcy's Story...

At the first hint of spring, I made my way to London with my sister and her companion. Georgiana was anxious to resume her music studies, and our aunt the Countess of Matlock wished to begin her preparations for a coming-out. My sister and I had decided Georgiana's debut would take place in the little Season during the autumn. Wanting an enormous show, neither of my aunts were pleased, but I remained adamant and even unbent enough to explain that putting a shy girl into a society crush and expecting her to shine would only lead to everyone's disappointment. A little Season was terrifying enough for Georgiana, but she had resolved to get the thing done as though she were planning to have a tooth drawn.

As February ended, my sister's mind must have turned toward this looming task and away from her curiosity about Elizabeth Bennet because that lady had not come up in conversation for some time.

Or so I thought. But the drive down the North Road to London is tedious, and during one stretch when her companion dozed, Georgiana abruptly asked, "Would Miss Elizabeth Bennet like me, do you think?"

Not having had to broach this subject recently, I struggled to comprehend the nature of her question. "Of course she would," I replied impatiently.

"Would she think my manners at fault? Would she think I, too, am proud and disagreeable?"

Apparently, I was mistaken. My sister's fascination with the lady had gone unabated, and she had obviously harbored this question for some time. Rather than bluntly saying that I doubted she would ever meet the lady and that Elizabeth Bennet's opinion of us hardly mattered, I was forced to think for a moment.

"Miss Elizabeth is not cruel, and moreover, she is perceptive enough to see shyness as the source of your reserve. In *my* reserve, she saw arrogance, and even then, she only teased me for it." I briefly remembered the lady's dark, twinkling eyes and the unaffected way she spoke to her friends. "Given half a chance to know you, I believe she would like you very much."

After five miles of silence, my sister asked, "But are we not very rich, William?"

What the devil? "We are well enough," I said irritably. "What do you mean?"

"I have been thinking," she began, looking over to make sure Mrs. Annesley was indeed asleep. "Your objections to Miss Elizabeth are that her family has connections in trade, that she has no fortune, and that her family is not always well behaved."

"Yes," I said with a finality that was meant to convince me as much as my sister.

Georgiana, undeterred, began to speak to me in the tone of a barrister at court. "But her relations cannot really matter. If poor connections were an impediment to mixing, then you would not be friends with Mr. Bingley, and you would not let Miss Bingley make eyes at you."

Before I could defend myself on this count, she went on. "And as to relations who are not always well behaved, you must own that Lady

Catherine's manners are atrocious, and Lord Matlock drinks himself into a state with regularity. The countess has made an art of snubbing almost everyone because of her rank, and Cousin Anne never speaks, which is excused because she is sickly but is rude nonetheless. And our oldest cousin, John, is a useless fribble, or so says Richard."

She took a breath and looked at her hands. "My own behavior must also be considered," she added in a whisper before gaining momentum and looking at me directly, "and we must own we are neither of us perfect in our manners."

She gathered her resolve before her thundering conclusion, which poured out in the artless voice of a young girl. "And that leaves only your objection to Miss Elizabeth's lack of fortune, so I have to wonder whether we are in difficulty. If so, you may take my dowry away, William, and then perhaps you can marry where you like."

Marry where I like? I could hardly think how to answer this, so I deflected. "You do not want your dowry, love?"

"Laugh at me if you like," she said gravely, "but I would trade my position any day for that of Miss Elizabeth. If a man were to offer for her, she would know he did so because of her merits or from affection, but I shall never have such certainty."

We hit a bump at the instant my sister ended her sentence, and Mrs. Annesley, rousing herself, sat up. This unfortunate interruption left me to stew over all my sister's confidences.

Like a cow ruminates on grass for days and days, I ruminated on my sister's guileless suppositions, but I came to no clarity. The matter of Miss Elizabeth's eligibility was purely hypothetical because, short of arriving in Hertfordshire for the purpose of courting her, I would never see her again—not to mention the hostility with which we parted! I sincerely hoped my sister would forget I ever mentioned the young lady in the first place, and I departed for Kent resolved to think of other things.

My coach went first to Surrey to the Brigade of Guards at Pirbright where I collected my cousin Richard, and from there, we went on our annual Easter pilgrimage to Rosings Park, home of Lady Catherine de Bourgh. We did not go willingly, but we had been told to go from the age of our majority by the lady's brother, Richard's father, and my uncle: the Earl of Matlock. Our instructions were to make sure she did not 'ruin the place.' The visit was an aggravating duty, and if not for my cousin's company, it would have been unbearable.

A colonel in the brigade, Richard was near me in age and as close as a brother. He had spent the bulk of his formative years with my father and me at Pemberley while his own father focused on bringing his feckless heir 'up to snuff.' Wickham, meanwhile, had been part of our confederacy of youth, and we fell immediately to speaking of him as we made our way into Kent.

"He has gone to Jamaica," my cousin said with a note of satisfaction.

"Is that so? I wonder how he managed to get away. The tipstaffs are rarely casual when they have a man cornered."

"He stole a horse and took the back road. One of his friends tipped him that two burly chaps got off the mail that morning in Meryton asking after him."

"If he stole a horse, he can hardly expect to resurface respectably."

"No. I do not think he fancies being hung by the neck. He took pauper's passage on the first ship to leave Bristol, which happened to be on the sugar run."

"Jamaica! I shudder to think of the mischief he could do in such a place."

"Without a decent change of clothes or anyone who has heard of the Darcys of Pemberley? No. He used you and his oily manners as his pass card of respectability. Without that, he is just another dirty pilgrim. He could not have gone with more than the shirt on his back."

"Is my sister safe, then?"

"I am going to say with certainty, yes. Think no more on Wickham, and if you are still uneasy, then I shall write to the commanding officer in Kingston to tell him of a horse-thieving deserter who took passage there. Now may we turn the page, Darcy? What have you been doing?"

I longed to tell Richard of my flirtation with Elizabeth Bennet and its unhappy ending. My sister's pressing on this nerve would also have been on my list of confidences since Richard shares guardianship of Georgiana, and his sense and wisdom with regard to her would have helped me. But my reserve, almost inborn, would not allow me to confide even in a man so close to me. Not yet, not while I still thought of Elizabeth with alarming constancy.

Elizabeth! Just when had I begun to think of her in such an intimate way?

Perhaps, when she became a comfortable object in memory, I would no longer think of her as 'Elizabeth.' Then I would be able to tell Richard about her and receive his inevitable teasing with calm amusement.

And so, I glossed over my visit to Hertfordshire, entertained him with descriptions of Miss Bingley's attempts to ensnare me, and gave him the details of our plans for Georgiana's presentation. He spoke of the war, of course, and of his brother's uncanny knack of running through the family fortune at the races. His own prospects were secure. He had scrimped and saved and had enough for a modest property outside his family's grasp so that, when he eventually sold out, he could watch the earldom die from a distance.

"As bad as that?" I asked in alarm.

He shrugged. "There has always been more show than substance. Matlock earls have managed to hollow out the fortune from below, leaving the crust still glittering. My father had not your father's sense or determination to do more for his heirs than was done for him. But ours is not the only family to live on air. Fifty years from now, I wonder what will be left of the peerage."

"This is indeed an uplifting conversation. I hope you are half as charming when we are confined to Lady Catherine's parlor."

He laughed. "Do not mistake me. I am more hopeful than I have been. Having decided to do for myself, I find the future a comfortable prospect."

"Where will you settle?"

"I shall look around. Nothing large, mind. Perhaps, like Bingley, I shall find a nice country estate somewhere and grow barley. Or I might find something in horse country. Will you look into it for me? You have an eye for these things."

"I shall begin the search tomorrow. And if you are smart, you will let me teach you what to do with a plot of ground. Or a string of horses, or a flock of sheep."

He laughed and sat back with a contented look on his face, a look that struck me as far *too* content to derive from a modest property.

"Never tell me you are in love, Richard," I said with a sudden burst of percipience.

"No, no, but I am free to fall into it now that I have decided my own future, and I find myself quite ready to start a family."

Chapter 13

Rosings Park

We made the turn from Hunsford Village to the gatehouse of Rosings and passed the parsonage on the left. Since I happened to be seated on that side of the coach, I saw Mr. Collins in his front garden bowing and waving like a pestilential flag. Next to him stood three ladies, and one of them, I would have sworn, looked like—

"What is it, Darcy?" Richard asked when I sat up abruptly on an inward-drawn breath and nearly hit my head on the roof.

I struggled to regain my composure. "Nothing—only my posterior is beginning to suffer from so much travel. I shall be very glad of a walk."

"Which you will not get. We shall be dragged into the parlor to stand in front of Black Annis while she sharpens her iron nails."

I remained unsettled, but Richard's joke distracted me. When we were boys, we referred to Lady Catherine as Black Annis, a witch of lore who ate lambs and children and hung their skins outside her hut. Our relation was, in truth, a self-consequent bore, and before I could think, we were making our bows in front of her as she sat in an elevated chair with a faded velvet footstool.

No sooner had we said what was required than our cousin Anne was called. She dragged herself forward with a great show of suffering before wordlessly sinking in her chair and looking at us in a pucker of resentment. Whether the girl was truly ill or only ruined by such a stupid mother I could not decide. In either case, she was an awkward occupant of any room, for she refused to speak if she could avoid it.

"I see you look at Anne, Darcy," Lady Catherine said with satisfaction. "She has improved, has she not?"

Road weary as I was, I had not the temper to play this game. I turned to my cousin and said, "Have you improved Anne? Are you feeling stouter this year?"

This was not the *improvement* my aunt had in mind for me to notice, and she sought to bring attention back to herself by trying another tack.

"We shall have company for tea. My parson has married, and his wife's sister and friend from Hertfordshire visit. With Mrs. Jenkinson and both of you, we shall fill out two card tables. I do not let Mr. Collins play. Darcy, you will sit at Anne's table. Anne, you *will* play," she said as she motioned for her butler. "Benson, see the tables put up before tea."

Struck perfectly dumb, I sat for a quarter of an hour as mute as Anne, leaving Richard to shoulder the burden of entertaining my aunt. Once released to refresh myself, I staggered up to my room. My mind reeled, my body thrummed with anxious disbelief, and the words, "Elizabeth. Married!" ran round and round in my head.

Then I knew what I had refused to admit before. I harbored some idea of having the lady myself. Not only did I harbor this notion, I had come to regard it as a settled course, and worse, like any self-possessed savage, I had become overtly possessive of *my woman*.

My own unacknowledged passion and the worm of Georgiana's arguments had woven into the base of my skull, and like the Matlock fortune, my objections were eaten away from below, leaving only a thin veneer of reasonable denial on the surface. The shock remained for some minutes, but it was soon overtaken by rage that, illogically, I directed at the lady in question.

How could she demean herself and marry that posing, bumptious idiot? What joy would she gain in producing sons and daughters with such a man? They would be mealy little beasts, and the getting of them—! I nearly retched to picture her lying beneath the flailing buttocks of such a pig.

I had absolutely no plan in mind, but I wrenched off my travel clothes and put on the garb of a country gentleman out on an errand of murder: buckskin breeches, black frock coat, and my second-best boots. My valet could not smirk at me for whistling now, I thought darkly as I scowled at him.

"Briskly, Carsten. I am not dressing for a ball. Tell the colonel I am walking off a cramp, and if he is lucky, I shall be here in time for tea."

I stormed out the south-side door, an exit my aunt did not haunt, wove my way around the house, and moved at a stiff march toward the parsonage. What I meant to say to Elizabeth Bennet was in the nature of, "How *could* you!" The tone I meant to use was the roar of a bull on the charge. I was close to snorting when I arrived and stormed into the parlor where sat my woman, my betrayer, my love. Barely noticing the other ladies in the room, I bowed reflexively, and suddenly, I could think of nothing to say. Blank. Bug-eyed. Panting and stricken.

"Mr. Darcy!" Charlotte Lucas gasped upon my abrupt arrival. The ladies curtseyed, and I bowed again, still unable to make my jaw move.

"You are very welcome, sir. Will you have a seat?" Charlotte Lucas still spoke, which struck me as strange, but my head was benumbed, and I sat. "You remember my sister, Maria? And Miss Elizabeth and Miss Mary Bennet?"

Finally, I mustered the courage to look at my woman, the woman I had stupidly forfeited for—

Wait! "Miss Elizabeth?" I asked fuzzily.

"Mr. Darcy," she said with concern written on her face at my strange manners. "I did not know you were in Kent, sir."

"My aunt," I mumbled. My tongue felt foreign like a link of sausage lodged between my teeth.

"Lady Catherine has both nephews to visit her at Easter every year, Eliza," Charlotte Lucas explained, and thinking the conversation was as bad as it could be, I looked up and saw Mr. Collins enter the room.

"Mr. Darcy! What condescension, sir, what a compliment!" He babbled at me for a full minute. I heard nothing he said. Suddenly the room was silent, and I knew my turn to speak had come.

"I wish you joy on your marriage," I said to him woodenly.

"Yes, yes. My dear Charlotte," he said, putting a hand on Miss Lucas's shoulder, "has made me very happy."

The room again went silent, and I looked for the first time at what was presented to me. Charlotte Lucas sat in a place of prominence by a tea tray, and Mr. Collins stood smugly behind her, while Elizabeth, Mary Bennet, and Maria Lucas sat on a pretentious little settee.

"Congratulations, sir, Mrs. Collins," I said again in a colorless voice. And then without preamble, I turned to my object.

"Miss Elizabeth, the grounds at Rosings are known for their walking paths. Might I show you a passable lane you would like?"

She stood briskly. "I would be grateful for a walk, Mr. Darcy." She glanced at her sister Mary and said something with her eyes, which I took to mean she did not wish for company. "Charlotte," she said, turning to Mrs. Collins, "might you spare me half an hour?"

"Of course. I know you love a walk." She turned to me and said serenely, "You are kind to think of my friend, sir."

Mr. Collins looked perplexed and might have objected at my going with his cousin unchaperoned, but his new wife turned to him and said, "Will you find Papa and let him know Mr. Darcy has called? He will want to greet him after his little walk with Eliza."

"Is Sir William with you?" I asked, still slightly stupid. "I shall be very happy to greet him."

Elizabeth's Story...
MR. DARCY! IN KENT!

He walked me as one walks a dog or a horse—that is to say perfunctorily—up a pretty lane lined with limes and small wood just starting to show green. We went forward—tense, brisk, and silent. At last I could contain myself no longer.

"Was that your notion of a bride visit?" I asked sternly.

He stopped abruptly and turned to face me in an attitude of fury. "I thought you had married Mr. Collins."

"I?" I, too, came to a furious halt and turned to face him.

"My aunt said he had married and that his new wife's sister visited him from Hertfordshire. What was I to think? I saw you standing next to Mr. Collins with your sister when we passed in the carriage and I-I thought you—"

"And you arrived at the parsonage to—to what end, sir? To remonstrate with me for marrying my cousin?"

"For marrying a toad, yes. I credited you with a stiffer backbone."

I turned away to continue my much-needed walk. "Well!" I said in a huff.

"Indeed."

His ill humor amused me, and my anger died as suddenly as it had flared. "A lucky escape," I said sweetly to tease him.

"Yes."

"I think you would have beaten me, sir."

"I might have. There is nothing I hate more than waste, and you would be wasted on that man."

At last, I laughed. It began as a sort of reluctant chuckle and ended in a chortle of mirth. "Come, Mr. Darcy," I said eventually, "you must be diverted at least a little!"

He looked at me with his mouth still stiff and puckered. "I find nothing diverting at all in my mistake."

"Oh," I said lightly. "I had forgot. You are *not* a man who makes mistakes. Well then, I shall retreat into grim silence, and we shall march up this hill."

The most reluctant, begrudging grin peeked out, and he held out his arm to me. I took it, and we did walk, then, for a good distance in total silence. The exercise was not unpleasant. In fact, I felt myself falling deeply in love with this haughty, broodingly superior man.

At a crossroad where our path met a lane, we paused to let a little phaeton and pony go by. I noticed a lumpy figure reclining on the bench while a liveried servant held the reins. Mr. Darcy looked slightly piqued by this person's passing, and so, breaking our silence, I asked him in my lightest imitation of a busybody, "And who was that, sir?"

He turned to me with the shadow of a smile in his eyes. "That," he said flatly, "is the woman my aunt intends me to marry."

"That is Miss de Bourgh?" I could hardly disguise the surprise—nay, the objection—in my voice.

"My cousin Anne."

"And are you indeed going to marry her, sir?"

He looked at me again, and this time the smile in his eyes was unmistakable. "I would as soon run away with the goose girl."

My heart swelled despite my every inclination not to rejoice. We turned back to the parsonage, and after a quarter of a mile, I said, "Mr. Collins speaks of your engagement as an acknowledged fact."

"Does he?" he asked sharply.

I nodded, and he subsided into silence as though pondering. "My aunt's doing, I am sure. I suppose she has told anyone and everyone that we are promised."

"What will you do?"

"Disabuse her of her fancies. But not until I am poised to leave. There will be an uproar, to be sure."

"Dear me! I hope to be long gone."

He gave me a queer little look, and we arrived back at the parsonage. Mr. Darcy made himself oddly agreeable to Sir William, spoke lightly to Charlotte, and frittered away the half an hour remaining before we left to take tea at Rosings.

He accompanied us in an unprecedented show of gentlemanly behavior. We went in pairs. Mr. Collins and Charlotte led the way, followed by Sir William and Maria, with Mary and me bringing up the rear. Mr. Darcy began with the Collinses, but as we walked, he drifted back to Sir William, and then to us. I nearly jumped when he spoke to my sister Mary for the first time in our acquaintance.

"Miss Mary, how have you found Kent?"

"Enjoyable, sir, thank you."

"And your family? Are all well at Longbourn?"

"Yes, sir. We prepare for a wedding in June."

"Do you?"

"My sister Jane will marry Mr. Bromley, a doctor from London. Do you know him, sir?"

I smiled at Mary's naïve idea that society in London was so small that everyone would likely have met, but at the same time, I braced for Mr. Darcy to make some cutting remark for which I would have to throttle him.

He glanced once at me and said, with surprising gentleness, "I have not had that pleasure. Have you met my aunt, Miss Mary?"

"No sir. We are to be introduced to her this afternoon."

"You will, I hope, overlook her worst manners."

Mary looked at him in surprise. "Of course, sir!"

Mr. Darcy gave me a sidelong look. "I only hope your sister does not decide to take her on. She is a bit of a gorgon."

"I am perfectly capable of sitting still as a mouse while the lioness roars at us," I said firmly.

"Then I shall have seen something I would not have thought possible," he said with the ghost of a grin, "for I have been under the impression that the only lioness hereabouts is the one from Hertfordshire."

Mr. Darcy's Story...
I HAD GONE TOTALLY MAD.

Not only had I flown to the parsonage in a red-eyed rage, I had floated back to my aunt's dismal mansion in a giddy haze. The urge to release a whoop of joy and dance a jig around the room nearly overwhelmed me.

Sitting still was impossible. I paced to and fro before the window while I struggled for supremacy over surges of undirected energy that strained for release.

Lady Catherine did not notice me at first. She was in her element, lording over poor Sir William Lucas and his frightened younger daughter Maria. Her efforts to overpower the Bennet sisters, however, fell flat.

The ladies said everything perfectly but without inflections of awe. Their curtseys were respectful but hardly deep, and though they looked around the rooms appraisingly, they were visibly unimpressed by all the gilt and crystal. Elizabeth, I noticed, was careful to speak sparingly, and Mary, well, I could hardly credit she was the same girl known to me in Hertfordshire. They were ladylike, I concluded— both of them.

Finally, the tea tray arrived. "Mrs. Collins, pour the tea," my aunt commanded.

Mr. Collins jumped to his feet as though he meant to stand behind his wife and hurry her along in this duty, and unequal to watching a pantomime of inanity, I turned away. Behind me, I could hear Richard approach the Bennet sisters.

"My cousin Darcy was recently in Hertfordshire," he said in a conversational gambit. "Did you happen to meet him there?"

"We had that pleasure, yes," Elizabeth said in a soft voice.

"And what did you make of him, Miss Elizabeth?" Richard pressed with a hint of laughter in his voice. He enjoys teasing me when he can.

I held my breath to better hear her speak, but alas, I shall never know what she would have said of me.

"Fitzwilliam, of what are you talking? If you are in conversation, you must speak louder. I must have my share of what you are saying! Well, Miss Elizabeth? Miss Mary? What is my nephew telling you?"

Lady Catherine's strident demand grated on my stretched nerves as would Black Annis's iron nails, and I barked at her in anger.

"They were speaking of having made my acquaintance in Hertford-shire. Richard wished to know whether we had met."

"And did you? Did you meet my nephew, Miss Elizabeth?"

"Indeed, ma'am. He visited an estate not three miles from my father's property. I saw him at Sir William Lucas's home and at a ball at Netherfield." The tone of Elizabeth's voice was pitched to betray nothing but the most casual introduction between unrelated persons.

Sir William, hearing an opportunity to be amiable, then interjected a rambling observation of my general excellence. I glanced at the Bennet sisters with reddened ears while the man shoveled heaps of unearned praise on my head, and when Elizabeth met my eyes just once with a twinkle of pure irony, I settled.

She and I were in perfect accord; her look told me so. I took a breath, pushed away from the window, and found a seat near Anne. Lady Catherine, thrown successfully off the scent of the only real danger in the room, then turned away from the Bennet sisters and ignored them entirely for the rest of the visit. Richard, too, seemed to know that he ought not to expose them to the scrutiny of our aunt by his attention, and he moved away to speak to Sir William. Elizabeth sat back and shared a look with Miss Mary, fulsome of affection, support, and strength.

Then and there, under the watchful gaze of Black Annis herself, what had been mere passion for Elizabeth Bennet solidified into unyielding devotion.

How Georgiana would thrive under the umbrella of such a woman's affection! Lord, how *I* would thrive in the sphere of her influence! Determined to have her, I began to think of securing her at the first opportunity.

The afternoon progressed at a glacial pace. The company departed with an invitation to dine in three days, Richard left to write letters, and I went to the steward's room to make sense of his account books. Dinner, held at the fashionable hour of town rather than country, subjected us to Lady Catherine's unrelenting opinions on every subject known to man.

"Kill me," I mouthed to Richard from across the table.

He caught the butler's attention and had him pour me another glass of claret.

"I see you are enjoying the wine," Lady Catherine said to neither of us in particular. Neither of us replied because long experience had told us no reply was needed.

"My cellar is considered to be the best in Kent. I have always had excellent taste in these things. Sir Lewis used to compliment me for my selections, did he not Benson?"

Lewis de Bourgh was a drunkard, which explained both his ability to be married to my aunt and his early escape from her on account of dropsy.

"I have a large collection of French wine from before the war," she droned on. "Speaking of the war, why have you not won it yet, Fitzwilliam? If I could but get Wellington's ear for half an hour, I would tell him what should be done about it."

By the time she took her sullen daughter and Mrs. Jenkinson away, I sank my head on the back rail of my chair in exhaustion. Richard, too, fell back in his chair and sprawled out his legs. We sat for three quarters of an hour in blessed, stupefied silence.

"We had better go to the parlor," I mumbled eventually.

"I cannot do it, Darcy. I cannot. If she says one more word about Wellington, I am afraid I shall knock her down. When do we leave?"

Leave Kent? No! I sat straight up in my chair as though doused by a bucket of cold water. "Come," I said bracingly. "We are only unused to her ways. In no time we shall listen to her as one does a stream burbling over stones. Is that not how we have managed year upon year?"

"I can only do it if I am dead drunk. Pass me the port."

"Well, drink that and tell Benson to put brandy in your coffee. I need you to steel yourself for my sake."

Midway through his tall measure of port, my cousin looked at me and put his glass down. "Need me…?"

"Never mind," I said. "Can you walk without staggering?"

"I am a *soldier*, Darcy. I can sleep while marching. If we must go, then let us be at it."

Chapter 14

Elizabeth's Story…

Having heard Mr. Collins talk endlessly of her, I had suspected Lady Catherine de Bourgh was a character straight from Rowlandson's satirical pen. In reality, she *was* a flesh-and-blood caricature, and while I held my own under the gale force of her self-consequence, a particle of my mind fell to considering the inevitability of the decline of the British peerage if this lady was an example of its ranks. She was worse than ridiculous; she was ignorant and awful. Even Mr. Darcy applied himself to protecting my sister and me from her scrutiny, and poor Sir William, who bore the brunt of her focus, looked perfectly wrung out by the time we took our leave.

Since Mr. Collins's house was run like any other parsonage, by ten o'clock that night we were shut up in our rooms. Mary and I shared a modest bed, and I was happy to have company, lest I commence thinking of how to make myself fall out of love. My sister, however, decided we must speak of the one person I did not want to think about.

"What do you make of Mr. Darcy, Lizzy?"

Handsome, horrid, attractive, enraging, powerful, difficult, interesting, bewildering, educated, fastidious—the list unfurled in my head and looked to be a scroll one mile long. I jumped out from under the covers to get a slip of paper and a pen.

"I do not know what to make of him. Let us craft an exercise of your question."

Mary watched with curiosity as I tore the paper into eleven pieces. On each, I wrote the names of all who drank tea at Rosings. Then I smoothed the blanket and placed the pieces in a line.

"Wait," I said. I then made pieces of paper for our entire family, the Philipses and Gardiners included, and for good measure I made four more for the Bingleys and Hursts.

"Now," I said, "let us make a study of our acquaintances, shall we? Of all these people, who would you put above the rest?"

"Jane."

"Yes, of course. Shall we make a card for Mr. Bromley? They should go together."

Mary nodded. "Maria?"

"A babe. Sir William, too, in his way. They are innocents. Let us put them to the right of the angels, shall we?"

And so, we continued. Colonel Fitzwilliam had impressed Mary as a man of sense, and I could not disagree, so we put him to the left of the angels to designate a spot for the admirable mortals among us. I moved my Uncle Edward to keep the colonel company. Mary put our Aunt Madeline there as well.

"I do not know where to put Mrs. Jenkinson," I said.

"She and Charlotte must go together."

"Ah. Because they are both only trying to survive?"

The game became more challenging and more engaging as we sorted our little cards.

"Miss de Bourgh?" Mary asked.

"I do not know where she falls. What an inconsequential acquaintance!"

"I would put her with Mr. Hurst."

"You are very right. And Uncle Philips. Their use is that of filling a chair. Let us put them over there."

We were left with the more serious considerations and sat looking at the names before us in consternation. At last I said almost tentatively, "I hope you can forgive me, but I am afraid I must put Mama, our youngest sister Lydia, and Mr. Collins in a pile of embarrassing relations."

She held a knuckle tightly to her lips. "I feel guilty doing so, Lizzy."

"As do I, but really, they are all of a piece."

She nodded and spoke, also tentatively. "Should not Lady Catherine and Mr. Bingley's sisters be placed there as well?"

"Yes, along with Aunt Philips," I said, putting them together in an ignoble position under the inconsequential. "Let us call them… the poorly behaved? The irritants? The mortifying? Now, let us put Mr. Bingley somewhere too."

"He should go with our Uncle Phillips now that he has gone to London."

"Inconsequential—yes."

"Kitty?"

"I cannot put her with Mama just yet. There is something there that might be salvaged. Am I wrong?"

"If we could get her away from Lydia, I think she could find her way. She must have a place here between the sensible and the inconsequential."

"Yes. And now we must put Papa somewhere." Mary looked perplexed, so I made the decision. "He must go under the people of sense. He should be one of them, but he chooses to be contrary and to boast of his failures. He, too, must sit in a corner alone."

"You and I?" Mary asked.

"Exempt," I said forthrightly. "We are, after all, doing the exercise."

This left a lone scrap. "Now, Mary, where do we put Mr. Darcy?"

She thought for a moment. "He seems a man of sense."

"True. But the way he burst in upon Charlotte today was unforgivable."

"But he spoke to me this afternoon. Have you forgotten? He was very kind, I thought."

"Have *you* forgotten how pompous and overbearing he was when he was in Meryton?"

"But he sent a carriage for Jane when Mama was going to make her ride in the rain to catch Mr. Bingley," she said. "And you cannot forget how he came to your aid when you twisted your ankle."

"Well, there are few men who would leave a person fallen down on the road. You cannot deny the disturbing manner in which he paced in front of the window today when his aunt held court. I would not want to have him in my parlor acting the zoo animal."

"Lizzy, attend me. Mr. Darcy has nothing of Colonel Fitzwilliam's polished warmth or Mr. Bingley's amicability. There is no charm in any of his utterances, but one gets the sense that if he says something, he means it and, further, that his opinions are based on a foundation of intelligence, understanding, and education." I thought she was finished, but she continued. "Think of it! If Mr. Darcy were to tell you his opinion of Prime Minister Perceval, or of what should be done about the poor, or whether it was wiser to take this road or that when going to Bath, you would perforce listen to him."

"Yes, yes," I said, impatiently flicking his card with my index finger. "You want him in the pile of the sensible."

"I think he belongs right where he is—in the middle, standing alone. Who would not rely on him when hard-pressed? None of us. He is in a category apart."

"Do not tell me you are developing a fondness for him," I teased.

"I respect him a great deal, but I would like a more amiable sort if I dared to have a say."

"A Mr. Bingley for you, Mary?"

She wrinkled her nose and blew out her candle, leaving me just enough light to put our little cards in a pile and take them to the small coal stove in our room. I burnt us all up, even Mr. Darcy, though I shall admit he went in last of all.

Just as I blew out my candle and crawled into bed, Mary spoke in a sleepy drawl. "I think Colonel Fitzwilliam the ideal sort of man."

I smiled, tucked this confidence away, and resolved to try not to tease my sister for having made it.

MORNING CAME EARLY IN A PARSON'S HOME, AND I AWOKE TO A POUR-ing rain. Mary slept on, which allowed me to ponder my behavior.

I am a ninny, I concluded. How could I have fallen so weakly, pathetically, into the habit of pining for a man whose duty and conse-quence render me an unthinkable mate? How silly to think I could be safely in love with Mr. Darcy. I lay in bed in a tangle of confusion.

Are we not masters of our own feelings? Do our feelings make a right or left turn, swoop dizzyingly up and down hills, and take us willy-nilly into swamps and deserts without the slightest check from our rational minds?

Apparently.

The reality staggered me, and I rolled over in a bruised ache. Why had no one warned me to beware the temptation to fall in love? My father demeaned the king of emotions and teased me for being crossed in love. My mother's only notions of love have to do with securing a future. Even my Aunt Gardiner gave me no hint of the vicious danger to a person's heart of wild, rampant yearnings. She is secure in my uncle's regard, and he in hers. Between *them*, there is no painful disparity of feeling.

When my sister stirred, we lit our candles, such was the gloom of the day, and we dressed in a state of sobriety. Our morning looked to be deeply tedious.

"You will be missing your walk today," Mary said.

"And we shall both be missing our practice. Did you bring the Mozart? We can look at it at least and hear it in our minds."

"Lady Catherine has a pianoforte," Mary said wistfully.

"Yes, and I would wager it was last used when King Charles visited right before his execution. And even if we were invited to use it, which we never shall be, we cannot visit today, so we must brace ourselves for confinement in Mr. Collins's parlor—with Mr. Collins."

"Oh, I had not thought—I suppose he will not walk to the church today."

And he did not. Poor Charlotte wracked her brain for some means to keep her company entertained, but her husband decided we would enjoy a preview of his upcoming sermon. By ten in the morning, I felt the day should rightly be over. By the time tea was served, we fell on our refreshments with the voracity of beasts, simply for want of something to do.

With excitement, we greeted the sound of a carriage at the door. Had the bailiffs, the beadle, or even the undertaker come, we would have rejoiced at the interruption. When the maid announced Colonel Fitzwilliam and Mr. Darcy, a chorus of joyful welcome broke out.

They could not stay, Colonel Fitzwilliam said as spokesperson. Mr. Darcy stood by him looking grave. They were only passing on their way to look at the bridge on the north side of their aunt's property, and they wondered whether Sir William might like to come along. Word was the river was swelling dangerously, and they wished to decide for themselves whether the structure was sound.

The gentlemen left in a kind of dignified haste. Still, the breeze, tangy and cold, that came with them braced those of us they left behind. Charlotte and Maria glowed at the compliment paid to their father. Mary and I suddenly thought to practice our singing, and even the maid came to listen while she tidied the parlor. Newly inspired to preach about the great flood instead of the Leviticus he had planned, my cousin bustled off to read his Bible.

When the distinguished nephews returned, we must have looked much brighter, or so I hoped. Sir William certainly looked flush with importance, and when we asked after the flood, he said reports were much exaggerated. He huffed away to write a letter to Lady Lucas about his important adventure, and Charlotte, seeing her visitors standing damp from the rain, asked them to sit by the fire if they could spare the time.

The colonel looked once at his cousin and said, "We would be delighted, Mrs. Collins. Let me send the coach forward with news for Lady Catherine. The second team can come back for us if you can bear us for an hour."

"If you make it two, we shall bear it," I said lightly.

"Have you been as weary of confinement here at the parsonage as we have been at Rosings?" he asked.

"Indeed we have, sir," I replied as Charlotte went for hot water. Mr. Darcy stepped away to speak to his coachman.

"That cannot be, Miss Elizabeth. You have a liveliness here that we do not. Did you play cards?"

I paused as Mr. Darcy re-entered the room. "Mr. Collins does not play, sir. No, my sister and I sang for practice, which tells you of our desperation."

The colonel, it seemed, would speak for both men. Mr. Darcy held his jaw firmly shut and reminded me very much of the man I knew in Hertfordshire—taciturn, grave, and disinclined to make himself agreeable.

"I am sure you sing delightfully," said Colonel Fitzwilliam in his warm voice of spiced honey.

I laughed, and even Mary's face lightened into a self-conscious, blushing smile. "We are certainly delighted to make noise," I said, "but our audience might not be delighted to hear us, particularly if we are forced into a performance sans instrument."

We had stood long enough, and I motioned for our guests to be seated. Colonel Fitzwilliam sat by my sister.

"Is that the music you have been studying?" he asked.

"This is a Mozart my sister and I have been learning, sir," she said in a surprisingly demure voice. "For pianoforte."

"*Sonata facile*! My cousin, Darcy's sister, has played that for me."

"Elizabeth had a music master when she was in London this winter, and he brought it to her notice. Do you like it, sir?"

"You were in London?" Mr. Darcy barked the question.

As one, we swiveled to stare at his outburst.

"I went to have my ankle seen by a doctor, sir," I replied coldly. "My sister Jane went with me, and she liked my doctor very much more than I, it seems." I turned and said much more warmly, almost confidingly to the colonel, "They marry in June."

"How convenient to have a doctor in the family."

"His name is Bromley," Mary said. "Perhaps you have met him?"

My heart beamed at my sister. She had taken Jane's happiness so much to heart that she thought of Mr. Bromley as a kind of blessed figure to have entered our lives.

The colonel, who seemed to be improving into another blessed figure, indulged my sister. "I-I may have. I do not know. Tell me about him."

"He is young for such a learned man. He has red hair and blue eyes, and he has a marvelous way with our young cousins."

"Blue eyes you say?"

"Yes. Very blue," Mary said earnestly, unaware of being lightly teased.

"Do you know? He sounds vaguely familiar. My major, Johnson, had to be seen for a torn shoulder."

Mary nodded sagely. "Mr. Bromley did wonders for Lizzy's ankle."

Sensing Mr. Darcy's deep discomfort with the pace and tenor of this unenlightening conversation, I added to it with devilish pleasure. "He worked on a young cousin's thumb as well. He is a good man for joints, I think. Is your Major Johnson well healed now?"

"You had a music master?" Mr. Darcy asked in another burst of awkward inquiry.

Charlotte and Maria came in with the tea things, and their little commotion gave me time to swallow my ire. What a boor in a parlor Mr. Darcy could be!

"Mr. Finch came to my uncle's house in Cheapside. I understand he only made time for me because a distinguished pupil from Mayfair had gone into the country."

"Finch!" Colonel Fitzwilliam cried. "But this is marvelous. That girl was likely my cousin Georgiana."

"Oh?" I asked in a disinterested way, taking a teacup and handing it to Maria. "Charlotte, let me help you. Maria, be a dear and take this to your father."

Mr. Darcy subsided back into silence for the remainder of the visit. His cousin made himself agreeable and told Mary of the plays he had seen in London that year. He told me of the doings of his brigade, and he spoke generally of places he had travelled.

Mr. Darcy sat like a lump to be sure, but his cousin was a guest for the ages. When they stood to leave, I glanced coolly at the one and warmly at the other, but it was Mr. Darcy who took my hand and Mr. Darcy who held it overlong.

Chapter 15

Mr. Darcy's Story…

The elation and madness of yesterday lay dead in the cold, gray light of that rainy morning. I sat at a desk when I would much rather have ridden hard. I stared down at the blank page in front of me. Awake at dawn, I had thought to write to my uncle to tell him of my intention to marry Miss Elizabeth Bennet of Longbourn, Hertfordshire.

And there, under my drying pen, my aspirations came to a stuttering halt. I faced an assault of wild disapprobation from my relations. To marry a penniless nobody when my uncle's earldom teetered on the brink of insolvency would earn me no quarter. I could not be expected to fund their rescue, but as a wealthy connection, they would be extended more credit than otherwise. Were I to provide both wealthy and *noble* connections, the veneer of Matlock's consequence would shine all the brighter.

Relations in Cheapside and in the squalid village of Meryton would reflect upon them in exactly the opposite way. Any bride less than a titled heiress would disappoint. The duty, the obligation to family and service to its unrelenting hunger for power, for survival, had been pounded into me from infancy. Could I forsake this ancestral drumbeat? Black Annis would certainly hang my skin outside her hut if I offered for Elizabeth. Her howls would be heard as far away as London, and my uncle would hunt me down with all manner of threats—disownment, refusal to notice me, abhorrence of my wife and her children in perpetuity.

I thought the lady easily worth these consequences, but my family's rage would affect my sister, and therein lay the reason for my vacant stare at a blank page. There sat a letter I could not write.

I wandered the halls of Rosings in an interminable state of stupefaction. My disappointment physically hurt. I ached in every joint, every muscle, and I could not sit for ten minutes without standing abruptly. Richard found me haunting the billiards room, and we played an indifferent game. He tried to draw me out, but I could not be enticed to more than primitive grunts.

When a footman brought a note from the steward about the bridge north of Hunsford, my cousin said, "Thank God," under his breath, and we put on our caped greatcoats.

As we neared the parsonage, Richard hammered on the roof of the coach. I was too flooded with dismay to feel more when he suggested we invite Sir William to come on our errand.

"We face a deadly dull afternoon," he said, "and if we collect Sir William, we shall necessarily have to deposit him back again, and if we are asked to drink tea, we shall mop up a half an hour or more in consequence."

I faced Elizabeth, who now possessed my heart, as she sat across the room from me. What was left of me that day was the horrified, burnt out shell that had housed it for eight and twenty years. Could I live like this? I doubted I could, and yet what choice did I have? For what was my fortune, I wondered bitterly, if I could not have the woman I wanted most? In that wicked state of disenfranchisement, I briefly contemplated divesting myself of all my holdings to live like an ordinary man with a competence designed for a wife and two children.

Twice I betrayed my disconsolate state. "You were in London?" I blurted out to no purpose. And, "You had a music master?"

I sincerely hoped I could master my disappointment enough to forestall such blunderings when their party came to dinner on Wednesday, and for the most part, I managed a dignified silence unless directly addressed. My aunt carried the dinner conversation as was her prerogative, and since Sir William had returned home, she spent a considerable time asking the Bennet sisters all manner of invasive questions.

"What is your age, Miss Elizabeth?" she asked in her typically brusque fashion.

Elizabeth paused as though in disbelief at such a vulgar question before she answered coolly, "I am not one-and-twenty, Lady Catherine."

"And you?" she asked, turning to Miss Mary

"I am just turned nineteen, your ladyship."

The sisters exchanged one of their looks, and I knew Elizabeth was swallowing an urge to bluntly ask my aunt *her* age.

"There are five of you girls?"

Elizabeth took on the job of speaking. "Yes, ma'am."

"And I understand from Mr. Collins that they are all out?"

"True, Lady Catherine."

"Most singular," my aunt sniffed. "What was your mother thinking? Had I advised her, I would have told her to bring your younger sisters out only after her oldest daughters were married."

"I was not privy to my mother's logic, ma'am." Another look between sisters and I knew they enjoyed a secret joke in that their mother was not prone to either thinking or logic.

The casual and unintimidated manner in which Lady Catherine's interrogation was answered seemed to frustrate her. She turned abruptly to Mrs. Collins and introduced a new topic—that of the management of her poultry yard.

Richard, who was relegated to the nether regions of the table between Mary Bennet and Maria Lucas, spoke to them quietly. He managed, I noticed with envy, to pull modest smiles from Mary Bennet, and his efforts with Miss Lucas earned him shy looks of gratitude. My dinner companion, Anne, sat in a flaccid pile of shawls and sniffed into her handkerchief. The longer I sat next to my cousin and compared her to Elizabeth across the table, the more irate I became at the general family expectation I would marry Anne. There would be no possibility of heirs. None!

When we adjourned to the parlor, I stood at the mantle until the roar of the blaze forced me to move to the window. And when my aunt insisted we have music, I could not help but wander to the pianoforte where Miss Elizabeth sat, playing with expressive finesse. There was nothing I could say, and even if I had been equal to speaking in general that night, I would have been struck mute by the quality of her performance. Miss Mary, too, played well, and I wondered at my recollections of her plunking away as though she were chopping wood. The last chords of her rendition of Haydn rang pleasantly in the room.

"That was a passable performance," Lady Catherine called out from ten yards away. "I am an expert judge in matters of taste, and you should be pleased to hear me commend you. Anne, too, is very musical. I daresay if she had learnt to play, she would have been a prodigy."

Only Richard's hand on my shoulder restrained me from hurling the nearest object at hand at my aunt's head.

"Water running over stones, Darcy," my cousin murmured.

The next three days I spent in full retreat. Claiming the demands of my own estate's business, I closeted myself in my dead uncle's study, or I woke before Richard and went out with the steward to the farthest farms. If my cousin approached me with that look of his that signaled he was going to discover what ailed me, I forestalled him with busy talk of drainage and lambing.

I counted the days remaining in my tour of penance—twelve—and wondered whether I could become believably ill on Easter morning and forgo Mr. Collins's preaching on the Resurrection—and the sight of Elizabeth Bennet. And her company at dinner later. Unfortunately, I was never ill and did not quite know how to pretend to be. Besides, I was at heart a man, and a man does not cower in his bed.

Thinking to bring myself back to some semblance of my sensible self, albeit without my heart that now slept at the parsonage and took muddy walks in the woods, I began to think seriously of finding the time to disabuse my aunt of her matchmaking ideas.

The next day broke fine, and I thought the lanes might be dry, but in the midst of striding toward the stables with the notion of pondering while riding, a coach pulled up the gravel drive.

It looked odd to me. Was that—was that my own London coach? The one I left for my sister's use?

"Georgiana!" I roared. "What has happened?"

Chapter 16

Elizabeth's Story…

Our first inkling of news came at the sight of Anne de Bourgh's little phaeton and pony driving into the parsonage yard. The lady weakly handed Mr. Collins a note before waving at her groom to drive away. My cousin huffed and puffed into the parlor brandishing the paper in the air.

"Charlotte, my dear, we are to go to Rosings this afternoon!" He spoke in a fluster of anxiety intermixed with joy.

His wife replied with weary calm. "Are we, Mr. Collins?"

"Lady Catherine's niece has arrived—Miss Darcy! We are to have the honor of an introduction." He referred back to his note. "She is to go to church for the Easter service before returning to London."

"If that is the case, you might want to review your sermon. You will want the young lady's approbation."

When Mr. Collins dutifully ran to his study to do as she suggested, I asked, "Was Miss Darcy expected, Charlotte?"

"Not that I know of. Lady Catherine has often complained that Mr. Darcy does not bring her. Her visit is curious indeed."

And so, in the fashion of ducks on parade, Mr. Collins struck out with a long line of us behind as we made our pilgrimage to the great house for the purpose of bowing and curtseying to Mr. Darcy's sister.

I had mixed feelings, for Mr. Darcy had behaved in such a myriad of contradictory and disturbing ways since his arrival in Kent that I began to feel a strong resistance to meeting him. My curiosity, however, was aroused. I had heard from Mr. Wickham that Miss Darcy was as proud and disagreeable as her brother, but the Bingleys called her a sweet girl. In either case, the name 'Darcy' served as an irresistible enticement to me.

I expected a tall, strongly built, dark-haired and handsome girl modeled after her brother. In reality, Miss Darcy was tall for her age but not strikingly so, slender, and blonde. She wore an elegant dress and bore herself as though she had been trained to elegance rather than ease. In truth, her manners were as far from easy as her brother's were from loquacious. She blushed and stammered through introductions until she came to me, at which time, her blue eyes flew up to meet mine, and she cast such a searching look at me that I felt quite taken aback.

The ritual of tea began, and to our collective dismay, Lady Catherine demanded that Miss Darcy have the honor of pouring. No one could help her as she took her position by the teapot, alone in a public performance. That Lady Catherine began barking out instructions and corrections made the scene an agony. When the second cup chattered a little in its saucer and betrayed Miss Darcy's trembling hand, I went directly forward, took the cup, and passed it to Anne de Bourgh. I returned to help the girl, but Mary was before me, and we three made quick work of the tea.

The look we earned was one of unvarnished gratitude, and then I realized that Mr. Darcy's sister was indeed a shy girl whose natural reserve could give the impression of haughtiness, much like her brother.

Much like her brother! Was Mr. Darcy indeed uncomfortably shy behind the wall of his considerable consequence? Was he a man who was more at ease in the sparse company of intimates, a man who struggled to be sociable when in company? I thought of the times we had been alone and the way in which he nettled me and how often he made me laugh with real pleasure. Were he, indeed, seated on the high horse of his arrogance, he never would have lowered himself to entertain me.

I looked at him where he stood, strung too tight and ready to snap. He looked so watchfully at his sister that I thought, if he could do so without embarrassing her, he would wrap her in a blanket and carry her to the nursery to keep her safe from the world, safe from her horrid aunt. Well, he could do nothing for her in Lady Catherine's lair, but I could.

"Might you tell me, Lady Catherine, whether there is any truth to the rumor that your park boasts of a labyrinth?" I asked.

For a quarter of an hour, the woman's attention fixed upon educating me about Sir Lewis's pet project and away from her niece. When she seemed about to turn back to Miss Darcy, I spoke again.

"Did Sir Lewis model his maze after the Fontanellato in Parma, your ladyship? I have seen engravings of the pattern in a book."

She waved in annoyance. "The labyrinth at Rosings is twice as large as what the Italians could do."

"Twice as large? My word! The Fontanellato maze is spread over seventeen miles. Where is this wonder, Lady Catherine, and may I—would you indeed allow me the privilege of seeing it?" I spoke with enthusiasm and turned to Charlotte. "We could make a day of it. Certainly, it would require more than a day to navigate, but how delightful to walk a fraction of such a wonder!"

The weakness of a despot is the inability to be wrong about anything, and having come dangerously close to exposing Lady Catherine's ignorance, I earned the distinction of becoming her sworn enemy. Miss Darcy subsided into a meek pose so as to be invisible. Mary sat tense and still beside me, and Charlotte's expression became pinched with concern as Lady Catherine swelled up with wrath and rounded on me. Maria looked close to fainting.

"Seventeen miles? Bah, impossible! You should not believe anything written by an Italian, Miss Bennet. I do not know what your mother was thinking to have so neglected your education. I would be embarrassed to be in company, knowing as little as you do. And never—*never*—would I allow Anne even to stick her nose into a book about Italian doings. Foolish and vulgar country!"

Mr. Collins agreed in a righteous pucker. I smiled sweetly at him and then at my hostess.

"My ignorance has betrayed me, Lady Catherine. Do you indeed think the study of Italian is detrimental to a lady?"

I was enjoying myself immensely, but by the look of thunder on Lady Catherine's face, I thought perhaps I should not have gone so far as to trip her up a second time. I expected to be expelled from the room by force, but Mr. Darcy thought otherwise.

"The labyrinth of Rosings Park takes up a mere two miles, Miss Elizabeth," he said in the flat voice of the well-informed, "and the Fontanellato, according to my father whose grand tour included Parma, is the largest in the world. My own sister will have likely read about it. I have engaged an Italian master for her education since a lady must have some knowledge of the classic languages to be called accomplished. The man came recommended to me by the Duchess of Wessex."

"He is the shortest man I ever saw," Colonel Fitzwilliam interjected lightly.

"Is he? But I envy you, Miss Darcy. My sister Mary and I have dabbled in Italian but with little success. We began by attempting a very bad translation of Mozart's *The Shepherd King,* and alas, we ended our efforts there."

"*Figaro* was performed in London this year," Miss Darcy timidly offered. "I understood a little, at least."

"Did you like it? But how grand that must have been. Do you go to the opera often?"

"My brother takes me," she said in a fading voice. We were none of us unaware of Lady Catherine's growing outrage.

"Yes, but *I* took you to that one, Georgie," Colonel Fitzwilliam said in an overloud, jolly voice. "And yes, Miss Elizabeth, it was very grand if you enjoy caterwauling."

Our strategy was plainly to cut Lady Catherine completely out of the conversation. This was only possible because she was momentarily struck mute by my audacity.

"German operas are far superior," she said coldly upon recovering her voice. "When I was being courted by Sir Lewis, we took in a work of Handel."

"No, no, Aunt," the colonel said with a wink at Mary. "How can you say so? So harsh and guttural, not romantic at all."

Between Mr. Darcy, Colonel Fitzwilliam, and myself, we went about contradicting every statement Lady Catherine made until she called a halt to tea.

Standing abruptly, the great lady said, "Mr. Collins, go and prepare your sermon for tomorrow. I have no wish to see you—any of you— beforehand. There will be no dinner after, Mrs. Collins. You had better tell your cook to feed you. My niece is here, and we wish to dine as a private family party."

On the walk home, Mary and I dawdled behind. "You should not have antagonized her, Lizzy," my sister said in a low voice.

"I should not have, no. I fear I am now a pariah. So much for our fond hope of being invited to practice on her pianoforte. But at least Lady Catherine could not harry poor Miss Darcy when she was busy barking at me."

Chapter 17

Mr. Darcy's Story...

In a state of disordered tumult, I had escorted my sister down to take tea. Our conference upon her unexpected arrival had been conducted in the privacy of my apartment while a room was hastily readied for her. Richard came perforce, saying he would be in on our council of war, and Georgiana stood before us like a maiden bound for the guillotine.

"You will wonder what I am doing here," my sister said to her toes in a whisper of dread.

"'Wonder' is a mild description of what I feel. I am appalled. You should not travel alone and upon some mad whim without either of your guardians knowing where you go and for what purpose." Never mind that she came with a coachman, a groom, a footman, a maid, and her companion. To my mind, she may as well have run away on the common stage. "What are you about?" I demanded. "What was Mrs. Annesley about to let you come here?"

My sister's face paled, and I thought she might burst into tears. "Pray, William, do not blame her. I *made* her come because I said I would leave without her. She did not want to do it."

I grumbled. "Well? What is your emergency then, miss?" That must have hurt her. I had only called her 'miss' once before, and that was when she confessed her plan to elope with Wickham.

With her head bowed in pitiable dejection, my sister wordlessly pulled a paper from her sleeve and handed it to me. This was to be my explanation? A piece of paper? Good lord, had Wickham written her? I sat up in agitation, unfolded the letter, and read.

Dear Georgie,

We are safely in Kent, and Lady Catherine is as she ever was. Darcy, however, is as far from being as he ever was than I have known him to be. I suspect the cause is a visitor to the parsonage, a Miss Elizabeth Bennet. Your brother is behaving the idiot, which tells me all he will not say to me…

I read grimly through to the end of Richard's letter and looked up at my sister.

"Well?" I asked in stern disapproval.

"Come, Darcy," Richard said quietly. "Plainly, Georgiana came to meet Miss Elizabeth. You need not drag the confession from her. Were you curious as to who has caught your brother's notice, kitten?"

My sister nodded and flashed a look of gratitude at our cousin before her eyes rose to mine in an open plea for mercy.

"Very well," I said. "You will meet Miss Elizabeth this afternoon. There is no choice, but you must stay for church, and then I shall see you back to London." I spoke with uncharitable disinterest and added, for the sake of punishment, "And you will bear with Lady Catherine, for if you insist on coming to Rosings uninvited and unannounced, then you must be equal to her strictures."

Richard kissed her cheek and I, still fuming, said, "You may go and change before I take you down to tea. See that Mrs. Annesley is properly put up, as well as your footman and outriders."

Once we were alone, my cousin rounded on me. "Darcy," he said in the voice of a man intent upon talking sense into a fool.

"I shall not listen to anything you say, Richard."

He persisted. "Miss Elizabeth—"

"I shall most particularly not hear anything you say about Elizabeth Bennet."

We had then gone down to tea, and Elizabeth—my heart, my sister's rescuer—did that afternoon what I had never done, what I had never thought of doing. The exercise had been a revelation.

She challenged Lady Catherine de Bourgh, calling into question my aunt's benighted pronouncements and bearing the lady's rage with lighthearted indifference. I took up her cause. How could I not? Richard, too, joined in, and even Georgiana, meek as a lamb, ignored the witch in the room.

We disputed her distortion of facts and refused to be drawn in by her demands for attention, and when she furiously dismissed her visitors from the parsonage, I went forward to where she sat in a smoldering rage.

"That was badly done, Aunt."

She puffed up and replied, "I have never encountered such disrespect in my life. The impertinence of that girl! And you...you! To go against me!"

"You do nothing to earn her respect—my respect. Your manners in company are officious and unkind. I leave here Monday at first light with my sister. Do not expect me to wait upon you again, and forego your hopes of securing me for Anne. My future does not comingle with yours, Lady Catherine—on this you must be clear."

On that note of reprimand, said in the spirit of a man taken past his limit of endurance and with the finality I truly felt, I stormed out of the room. I heard my aunt gasp and also the footsteps behind me. Richard and Georgiana flanked my exit, and we went as one body to collect ourselves in the library. My aunt's wails of outrage followed us down the hall, and we shut the door in relief.

My sister and cousin were slightly shocked, as was I if I am honest. We stood in a strange, mute group, looking at one another until Richard spoke.

"A rupture, Darcy?"

"Apparently so. My breaking point came upon me unexpectedly. I shall never apologize for what is the mere truth. Are you angry with me?"

He considered the question. "You have borne a great deal from her."

"As have we all. And why? Why have we sat hour upon hour in sullen silence while she has berated us and spouted absurdities on every subject? I have seen—I have been *shown*—that we ought not to let a fool bully us into submission."

"Miss Bennet is very brave," my sister timidly put forward.

"Yes. That she is, Georgiana. But of her we must speak. I cannot offer for her—surely, you see that. If I were to marry her, our uncle would cut her, and in doing so, he would cut me. And you—I cannot ruin your future."

Suddenly, my normally diffident sister rose to stand at full attention. She spoke with an animation I had not heard in a long time. "But this is marvelous! I told you I do not want to be an heiress."

Richard frowned in confusion. "Not want to be an heiress? What is this nonsense?"

"I shall never know whether I am receiving an offer out of affection or ambition. Do you not see? If we are nameless with Lord and Lady Matlock, our consequence will tumble, and if I am courted, my suitor will necessarily partake of our fallen position. He would have to be stouthearted, do you not agree? For what is money without power? There are tradesmen by the dozens who have ten times our wealth and cannot secure a voucher at Almack's. I say this is marvelous," she concluded as stoutly as the beau of her imagination. "You must marry Elizabeth Bennet if you love her. For my sake!"

Over the course of an afternoon and evening closeted as we were, my sister's notion, which I rejected out of hand at first, began to take on a life of its own. We ate our dinner in the library, and the three of us spoke at length about the prospect of a future without the assurance of support from our relations in the peerage.

"We shall not be invited to the grandest balls," I said.

Richard laughed. "This is your objection?"

"Georgiana's coming out might not be well attended."

"Which suits me perfectly, William. I would like the smallest affair we can manage. Have I not always said so?"

"My wife will not be invited anywhere in London," I said at last, as though this were my final argument.

"But at Pemberley and in Derbyshire, she will be of the first consequence. Miss Elizabeth does not strike me as a lady who requires more than that. She was raised in the country, was she not?"

"She is at heart a country lass," I conceded.

My resolve crumbled a little as I thought of Elizabeth walking my grounds. How her heart would delight at such splendid paths, and she would strike out regardless of a drizzle, returning splattered with mud and shining like a lamp on a cloudy day.

No, Elizabeth would not covet diamonds. I would woo her with my woodlands.

I wavered. "But what of you, Richard? Will not your life be made uncomfortable? You will be placed squarely between the Darcys and the Fitzwilliams."

"I have always been more of a Darcy at heart. Have I not told you I mean to live independent of my father's estate? What do I care if they cut me because of my support of you? I shall marry to please myself and live to fulfill my own notions of usefulness. No, you cannot use me as an escape. Do you love her?"

"I do," I muttered in bewilderment as though just discovering this truth. "I have severed my connection to Rosings on account of her."

Georgiana, who sat in an abstracted state throughout this strange conversation, suddenly spoke up, catching me completely unawares. "But does she love you, William? I saw no particular regard."

Chapter 18

Elizabeth's Story...

Easter morning dawned over a bleak and sober household. Mr. Collins's state could only be described as severe. At the breakfast table, Charlotte sat unsmiling and Maria subdued as the silence fell heavily over us. Tension—boiled, fried, and tough as shoe leather—was the course upon which we were to break our fast.

Mary and I served ourselves quietly, and aside from, "Pass the cream, please," nothing was said. For such an outspoken person, I suddenly could think of nothing to say. But after a silence of five minutes that was so uncomfortable I could hardly swallow my food, I knew exactly what I *should* say—what I needed to say.

I cleared my throat. "Charlotte, I have put you and Mr. Collins in a terribly inconvenient position. I believe it would be best that Mary and I return to London tomorrow. I shall walk to the village first thing and secure a post chaise or perhaps tickets on the mail."

"Oh, Eliza—!" she began, and she might have suggested we only remain inconspicuous until the worst of Lady Catherine's ire had blown past us, but Mr. Collins had altogether different plans. His tone, when he spoke, was wrung dry of all sympathy.

"You may go today. The coaching inn does not close on the Sabbath."

I was taken aback. "They do not even close for Easter service, sir?"

"Surely, Monday morning is soon enough, Mr. Collins," Charlotte said quietly, and then she looked at me with all the discomfort, apology, and condemnation she must be feeling toward me, her guest who had ruined our visit, cut up her husband's peace, and now forced her to ask us to go.

"I am very sorry." I felt genuine remorse. What hubris to go at Lady Catherine! I should have seen how my perversity would fall upon my friend. "I never should have let my tongue get the better of me yesterday. Now, you will be more comfortable if Mary and I sit in the back of the church during service. We shall go ahead of you this morning so you need not be seen walking with us, and this afternoon we shall pack. A tray in our rooms will do us very well, Charlotte. I am sure, sir," I said directly to my bitterly aggrieved cousin, "that once we are gone, Lady Catherine will call for you to visit her as she always has."

Once we had gone upstairs to ready ourselves to walk to church, I also apologized to Mary.

"My lord, I have caused you such a miserable time here. I am truly sorry."

She stood behind me, fussing with my lace fichu. "Never mind, Lizzy. Do you not always say, 'think only of the past as it gives you pleasure'?"

"You will excuse me from ever thinking upon this morning again. Poor Charlotte! At least Mr. Collins is not a man to beat his wife for the sins of her company. We shall, all of us, have a very long day, I am afraid."

"Will you really secure us tickets on the mail?"

We were not of the first stare to be sure, but we had never been reduced to any mode of transportation so common. My bravado was all we had to see us through, and so I spoke bravely.

"If I must put us on the mail coach, of course I shall. Surely, you see we cannot stay long enough to send a note to our uncle to have us collected."

My sister's discomfort did not abate, and I shifted into a tone of reassurance meant to convince myself as much as Mary.

"We shall be safe enough, you know. We have each other, and if we do not have to hire our own post coach, which I doubt we can on short notice, we shall be free to go to the shops in London and buy trinkets for our sisters."

THE CHURCH SERVICE WAS NO LESS MISERABLE THAN OUR BREAKFAST had been. Mr. Collins, possessed of the emotional depth of a clam, did not know how to ingratiate himself with a patroness who glared daggers at him. In consequence, he spoke his homily in accents so stringent and with a feeling so acrid as to make the glories of the Resurrection sound rather tawdry. Mary, who loved church as a rule, sat beside me in a state of revulsion at his execution of the season's most celebrated story and stared down at her hands.

In contrast, I looked around me with dispassionate curiosity. The parishioners of Hunsford looked to be in varying degrees of somnolence, dreaming of their inevitable release from worship—and of their dinner to come, no doubt. Charlotte took up her position in the front on the right. Maria sat close as though for shelter, and they both looked to be on their most pious behavior to mollify Mr. Collins. Lady Catherine, her daughter, Anne, and her dutiful companion, Mrs. Jenkinson, sat in the principal family box on the left. The great lady's expression was a mask of contained rage, and I could not help but wonder how and why my little challenge of yesterday could so affect her.

My eyes went at last to Mr. Darcy, Miss Darcy, her companion, Mrs. Annesley, and Colonel Fitzwilliam. One would expect they would sit in the reserved family pew directly behind the de Bourghs, but they were in fact one row behind even that. What, I wondered, had happened in that quarter?

While I pondered this curiosity, I noticed that Miss Darcy held her head up rather prettily. In fact, their party displayed such casual dignity throughout Mr. Collins's dreadful preaching that some of my natural dislike of Mr. Darcy's arrogance fell away.

He had a wee right, at least, to be above his company, did he not? He *was* a cut above those of us who sat behind him in rows of ordinary imperfection. Even his flaws were spectacular. Who else in this church would dare to be so bluntly uncivil in a lady's parlor? Who would unapologetically refuse to reply to a stupid remark and look incredulous at being applied to for such a response? There sat a superior man. And beside him sat his superior family.

I straightened my spine to emulate their general stateliness and whispered to Mary, "Look how Miss Darcy bears up."

My sister then also sat up, and after a moment, she rearranged her face from a scowl of disgust to one of placid forbearance. Our new dignity served us well when the interminable ordeal shifted into the ritual of departure.

Lady Catherine, whose precedence demanded we remain standing in our pews until her party walked outside, gave me a look of such unadulterated malice as she passed by that I might have staggered without the example set for me by Mr. Darcy's party. They passed directly after Lady Catherine. Both gentlemen nodded their heads, and Miss Darcy looked imploringly our way as though to say she did not hate me as did her aunt.

My sister and I waited until Mr. Collins was seeing to the last of his parishioners before we slipped out the side door to walk through the village toward my cousin's house. As we went down the square upon which the church is located, I suddenly became aware of a carriage coming up behind us and pulling to a stop. Fearing Lady Catherine would open her window to spit at me, I was most pleasantly surprised when the coach door opened and Mr. Darcy stepped out.

"Good day, Miss Elizabeth, Miss Mary. My sister asked whether she might walk with you."

"Of course, sir," I replied with a helpless smile. "We would be very glad of her company."

Colonel Fitzwilliam stepped out then and handed down Miss Darcy and Mrs. Annesley, a plump and pleasant-faced woman who carried herself with genteel confidence.

"We shall send the carriage on ahead to Rosings and take a leisurely stroll if we might impose," he said.

I replied with a light laugh. "I wonder whether you should be seen with me. My cousin Collins is wiser and hangs back until we are out of sight."

The colonel let out a chuckle. "Oh, but we, too, are in the dog box, Miss Bennet."

"What? All of you? For my impertinence you are made to pay?" I asked in surprise, looking up at Mr. Darcy for confirmation.

He nodded gravely, but there shone a light in his eye I could not name. "We leave at first light," he said.

"Do you? But so do—please tell me, sir, that my poor manners of yesterday have not caused you to go."

"Your manners of yesterday were rather what mine should have been all along where my aunt is concerned," he said as Miss Darcy came forward.

His words perplexed me. What was he saying? But by then, we had begun to walk, and I could not ruminate on his meaning.

Because the path narrowed once it left the square and pointed toward the entrance to Rosings Park, we went two by two. Colonel Fitzwilliam stepped ahead with Mary, Mr. Darcy went with Mrs. Annesley, and Miss Darcy and I took up the rear. When she began to walk slower, I fell back naturally to match her stride, and soon enough, we were a few paces behind the others.

"Pray do not let our aunt's behavior reflect badly on us in your estimation," she said in a small voice wrung with anxiety.

I laughed aloud. "Oh, my dear Miss Darcy, were you to visit me at Longbourn, I would have to ask you to walk out with me, and I would turn to you in earnest application and say, "Pray, Miss Darcy, do not let my family's behavior reflect badly on me and my sisters Jane and Mary." She looked at me wonderingly, and I added, "Might we call it even and say no more about it? For who has relations that one and all do a person credit? No one! There is always a witch, an ogre, a drunk, or a fool hung somewhere on the family tree.

"We have the witch," she said with a shy smile.

"And I have a harvest of fools of which to boast. My cousin Collins just proved my point by preaching such a sermon today."

"It was dreadful. Forgive me, I should not have—"

"But it *was* dreadful. I thought Mary would walk out of the church in a huff! But look at her talking to the colonel. Your cousin brings out a conversant side to her that I have not seen. *He* is an admirable plum on your family tree."

Rather than pleased, she looked slightly downcast. "My brother, too, is an admirable man," she put forth tentatively, and then I knew that by admiring the one I had cast aspersions on the other, a slight in my shy new friend's estimation.

"I am sure he is," I said in a light, neutral voice because I could not in good faith praise him to the skies.

He had behaved so strangely while in Kent that I began to think of him as a man of unsteady temper. A *handsome* man of unsteady temper. For half a minute, I walked along and admired the cut of his coat, the posture of a lean, well-built man with his dark hair curled ever so fashionably over a starched and snowy-white cravat.

Thinking to distract myself from the object of my helpless fascination and to divert Miss Darcy from my lukewarm approbation of her brother, I then said, "You and I have something in common."

"Do we?" she asked in surprise.

"Mr. Finch."

"My music master?" she asked, and we then fell into an easy tête-à-tête about musical studies, which took us straight to the door of the parsonage.

Mr. Darcy's Story…

MY SISTER AND COUSIN BOTH WARNED ME AGAINST SPEAKING DIRECTLY to Elizabeth until I was in better odor with the lady. Circumspection, they said in their own inimitable ways, was required after the hash I had made of my every encounter with her while in Kent. I wished to tell them of our delectable encounters in Hertfordshire but fell silent upon recalling the final clash in which I had so rudely crushed her pretensions. Perhaps others knew better than I how to go about repairing the wreckage I had made of a courtship begun unwittingly and largely against my will.

And so, after church—an hour and a half of my life I shall never retrieve from the void—I forced myself to walk with Mrs. Annesley as we escorted Elizabeth and her sister to the parsonage.

This was hard labor. I heard Elizabeth speaking lightly with Georgiana and longed to hang back to simply listen to the sound of two women I love in animated conversation. I tried to focus on Richard and Mary Bennet as they walked ahead of me, speaking pleasantly and, at one point, arm in arm as a small rut cut across the path. Thinking perhaps I could take Elizabeth's arm, I looked back and saw that she had cajoled Georgiana into jumping the muddy spot together, and once again, I marveled at Elizabeth Bennet's delightfully unconventional approach to all things difficult.

I must have her!

This had become a constant howl inside me. But was it true she did not like me? I had reeled at the implication of my sister's artless observation, and I grimly recalled how strangely I had behaved in Mrs. Collins's parlor. Elizabeth would not overlook my failings to marry for material advantages alone. I could not expect to buy her with my fortune. She must at least respect and admire me in order to submit herself to the confinement of marriage. I had heard her say so at Netherfield.

My abstracted worrying came to a halt when we reached the parsonage. As we clustered there, Richard spoke up.

"I say, Darcy. Miss Mary has been telling me that she and Miss Elizabeth are also leaving tomorrow. They hope to hire a post coach or to secure tickets on the London mail, but I have been trying to convince her that we could easily take them up."

"Oh yes!" Georgiana cried. "Pray, do come with us."

I saw the stubborn slant of Elizabeth's mouth, and I knew what she would say before she spoke.

"We cannot possibly impose."

Circumspection be damned! I took Elizabeth's arm and firmly led her a few steps away.

"For once, will you let me do something for you? Think! We have six ladies and gentlemen going to London and two coaches in which to do it. For what reason do you insist upon traveling in a third? Besides, I shall not hear of you going on the mail. I forbid it," I huffed darkly. "In this I fully intend to be overbearing and officious and every other particularity you hate.

She raked me with her dangerous look of old—that sharp, amused, admiring twinkle in her eyes. She cocked her head to one side and delicately, deliberately, raised her right eyebrow.

"But what of your valet and Miss Darcy's maid? Do they not travel with you?"

"They travel separately, of course," I said, realizing too late how spoiled this dismissive answer made me sound. "You may upbraid me all you like for the privilege, but if you had seen my cousin's batman—he travels with us as well—you would know why I refuse to sit in a coach with him. He is over six feet tall, and I do not care to spend the day with my knees intermingled with those of another man."

She laughed. "Oh, so I am to acquiesce without demure, am I?"

"Precisely, though I know you dislike my brand of gallantry. If I could offer you passage on a lamb cart, I am sure you would rather, but that option is simply beyond my means. Now, if you please, consider your sister Mary—who is staring at you as hopefully as a spaniel in want of a walk—and do as I say. Be ready to leave this dark country by first light, madam." As I spoke, my eyes caressed her face—not tenderly but with ferocious, flaming ardor—and I willed her to submit to my protection.

"I am reminded of you putting me most unwillingly up on your horse, sir," she said with a slight blush. "But we shall be ready with our trunks on this doorstep. I thank you most sincerely for the trouble."

I took her hand and said in a low voice close to her ear, "You may only thank me for what you willingly take from me. I would wish you thought better of me, Miss Elizabeth."

My heart's beautiful eyes flew up to mine. Her color deepened, but she had nothing with which to counter my challenge.

Turning back to her sister, she said, "Well, Mary, it appears we go to London in style with Miss Darcy." Turning to my sister she added, "And we shall be delighted to enjoy your company."

Georgiana beamed her happiness, and after we took our leave, we walked into the park in a meandering way. There was no hurry to return to Rosings since our party would not sit down to dinner with my aunt. Later, after our trunks were packed, we feasted on a cold collation and played cards in the library, while Lady Catherine ate with Anne in grim silence.

Black Annis dined on loin of child in the gloomy cavern of her dining room. For the life of me, I could not find a particle of sympathy to spare for her lack of company.

Chapter 19

Elizabeth's Story…

The next morning Charlotte came with her candle and helped us to dress, and we did so quietly so as not to awaken Mr. Collins.

"Forgive me?" I nearly whispered to my friend.

She kissed my cheek and spoke quietly. "What a tempest in a teapot, Eliza. 'Tis already forgot." After a few moments, while buttoning Mary's dark-gray travel dress, Charlotte slanted a glance at me. "I wonder that Mr. Darcy is leaving so abruptly."

"I cannot enlighten you there," I replied while peering into the dimly lit mirror and trying to make something elegant of my hair.

"Colonel Fitzwilliam said that Mr. Darcy refuses to marry Miss de Bourgh," Mary said.

"Oh my," whispered Charlotte.

Oh my, indeed! "Take heart, my dear friend," I said. "Lady Catherine's displeasure, currently being spread equally between me and her recalcitrant nephew, will soon enough be focused solely on the death of that dream. She will be forced to busy herself finding a suitable husband for her daughter, and your husband will find himself in her good graces again."

"I do hope so," she said. "But how lucky for you to be taken up by Miss Darcy."

I opened the door to Charlotte's manservant who had come for our trunks. "Lucky indeed! Charlotte, I implore you not to infer anything in that quarter." We were in the hall, whispering now. "I see your sly look even in the dark," I said with great affection. "Now, return to your bed and tend to the wounds of my cousin's self-consequence. He must be shaken to his bones, the poor man."

With our shawls wrapped tightly around us and up to our chins, Mary and I sat on our small trunks in the dim light of early morning just as I had told Mr. Darcy we would. We were not left to sit in the cold for more than five minutes, but in that time, I observed to Mary that there was something biblical in being evicted from a place—at Easter, no less—and just when a person feels thoroughly horse-whipped off the premises, there arrives some magical means of transport to a brighter land.

"Hmm," she said, adorably mistaking my jest as a serious observation. "Like the Israelites in their Exodus from Egypt?"

I swallowed a hearty laugh. "Just so, Mary. I believe I hear the waters parting as we speak." And true enough, the unique symphony of sounds heard only when a coach and four approaches, caused us to stand and make ready to go to London.

Miss Darcy looked very young and sleepy as she sweetly welcomed us and Mr. Darcy handed us up. Mrs. Annesley, too, made us feel wanted by settling us with a lap rug and assuring our comfort without being oppressively maternal. The hour being so early, we spoke only sparsely in hushed tones, and as the wheels jolted us into forward progress, my heart leapt in relief. This was an exodus indeed, and our horses may as well have had wings, such was my sudden joy to be leaving Mr. Collins's oppressive house.

THE DAY BROKE FINE AND MATCHED OUR DAWNING COLLECTIVE merriment. Mr. Darcy's cavalcade, outfitted with very fine horses, meant we travelled at a lively pace. Normally, the speed would make for an uncomfortable ride, but our coach springs must have been of some superior design, for we were spared all but the worst bumps of the road.

The interior of Miss Darcy's coach was no less marvelous than the sophistication of its springs. We sat on tufted velvet with our feet resting delicately upon a woven wool runner. The brass fittings and the glass sparkled, and the snug-fitting door spared us the invasion of dust from the road. This superior mode of travel propelled me into my forbidden dream. I thought of the finer things that came perforce with that dream, and I thought of Mr. Darcy sitting in the coach just in front of us. I knew this was not mine to dream of; nonetheless, I succumbed to the delicious comfort of his protection and left the facing of reality for later.

The dreamlike quality of that soft spring day continued as we stopped in Maidstone to break our fast. Mr. Darcy stepped into the inn, and the entire place burst into activity on his behalf. Our party must have been expected, for the innkeeper himself took us to a private parlor with a large window overlooking the principle street. His wife then showed the ladies of the party to an unheard-of luxury—a room hired not to stay the night but for the sole purpose of our privacy as we refreshed ourselves.

Within ten minutes of coming into the parlor, three maids bearing trays of mouthwatering food arrived. For me there was no question of picking elegantly at my plate. I was ravenous. Our final meals at the parsonage were too uncomfortable to satisfy, and from the relish of my companions, I wondered whether meals at Rosings had been similarly devoid of enjoyment. Mr. Darcy chose thinly sliced sirloin of beef with eggs and plum cake, he drank coffee instead of tea, and he smiled indulgently at me when I chose the luxury of two cups of chocolate. I then piously ate my well-prepared eggs so as to justify the hot rolls with butter and jam that ended my meal.

Soon enough, our appetites were sated, and the innkeeper returned to supervise the clearing of the board and to ask how we found the fare. To my surprise, Mr. Darcy became positively charitable.

"You have outdone yourselves, Martin. Pray do tell Mrs. Martin that her effort in the kitchen never disappoints."

"And if she made this jam, you must add my compliments, sir," I added, casting an impish grin at Mary. My sister had become a little more perceptive, I think, because she instantly caught my meaning and smiled back at me.

"Come, come," Colonel Fitzwilliam tsk-tsked. "What is this hilarity between sisters about the jam?"

I opened my mouth to explain only to be beaten by Mary! "Oh, I am sure it is not so very funny, sir. It is only that my sister Jane was speaking romantically about her upcoming marriage and told us of her earnest ambition to learn to make jam."

"You must know, Colonel, that our Jane is beautiful, and she is also quite a gentle person. The notion of her standing intently over her pots with her spoons and her apron must strike a person as droll."

He smiled. "And you, Miss Elizabeth? Do you also wish to excel at jam making?"

"Upon no account, sir! If I am to excel at anything, it will have to be something far less useful. Mary is more likely to have any ambitions in the kitchen."

My sister blushed prettily and said she only ever wished to be useful somehow and that idleness, though fashionable, had never been one of her pleasures. The colonel seemed to like that answer very well, and he went on to badger Miss Darcy about her knowledge of cheese-making and the like until Mr. Darcy took pity on his sister and changed the subject.

The gentlemen fell to talking about the road and of our progress, and wishing to stretch my legs, I stood and went to the window. Miss Darcy asked after her wheeler, and the three then spoke of the merits of the teams.

Not having put much thought into our horses, I was surprised to learn the gentleman kept two teams on this road, for we would change again in Bromley. Gazing out the window, I stood in wonder at the depth of Mr. Darcy's fortune. We travelled in three carriages, so twelve fresh horses would be required twice over. And this was nothing to the hospitality of the house, not only for the six of us but also for his retainers that numbered nine together.

In a distracted and slightly discomposed state, I stared down at the street and wished I did not harbor such a fatal, irreversible fascination for an ineligible man. Only vaguely did I hear Colonel Fitzwilliam offer to take Mary for a little walk, and I positively jumped when Mr. Darcy spoke to me directly.

"I would have sworn that when we entered this room your eyes were all sparkles."

"Excuse me?" I asked, turning back to the room in bewilderment. Mr. Darcy stood, arms crossed, with one shoulder against the wall as he examined me; belatedly, I realized we were alone.

"I would know what troubles you," he said bluntly.

"What makes you believe I am troubled?" This sort of diversionary feint I had learnt from Papa.

"You have stood at that window in deep, dark thought for five full minutes. While that is one of my favorite pastimes, I do not believe it very like you to brood. What troubles you?"

I am in love with you, I thought. But aloud, I said, "I have been thinking of horses."

"Horses!"

"Yes, horses. How many do you have on this road—twenty-four?"

"Twenty-four horses? Of what are you talking?" He was speaking to me in that way I love—sharp, impatient and devoid of condescension.

"You have three carriages."

"Oh. The service coach uses job horses. I suppose that is somehow a form of snobbery in your estimation. But in fact, I have eight horses on this road when I travel to Kent. My sister's coachman necessarily sent along two strings as well for her when she left London. They are collected and either stabled in London or placed on the road north when I go to Pemberley." He paused as if debating before he hardened his jaw. "I have three more teams from Pemberley that, along with this string, I put at coaching inns along that route. I have eight horses for riding in London and my estate. My sister has half a dozen, and we stable a strong team for estate work as well as our elderly stock in pasture. There are fifty-odd all totaled in my stables, and now you know the whole of it."

He stood and spoke as one who dared me to despise him for his honest confession, and when I did not reply, he raised his eyebrows and made an impatient motion with his head demanding I explain my objection to the size of his stable.

"You intimidate me, sir," I admitted in a small voice.

Mr. Darcy's Story...

"YOU INTIMIDATE ME," SHE MURMURED.

We were alone, arguing about horses of all things. She objected to my keeping horses on the road, or so I thought. But with those three words, a light came on in my head, and I became slightly irate.

"No," I snapped at her. "You have poked at, laughed at, and punctured my consequence from the first moment of our acquaintance and done me a great deal of good in doing so. You may not *now* express awe at the size of my stables."

A small, reluctant smile peeked out though her eyes remained modestly downcast. I pressed on.

"You, Elizabeth Bennet, are equal to anything. You have defied Lady Catherine de Bourgh, and if you do not stand up to my wealth and consequence and the many privileges I enjoy, if you do not take in your stride what service I offer you out of friendship, then I shall…" I faltered, uncrossed my arms, and came across the room to stand opposite her. How could I tell her of my disappointment if she proved not to be the woman I believed her to be?

"You will what?" she asked with her head tilted, sparrow-like.

"Nothing! You are *not* a wilting, cringing miss styled after Maria Lucas. I refuse to believe you are, and this talk of my horses and intimidation is pure silliness."

Elizabeth's face softened as a tender smile broke out and the sparkle returned to her eyes. "You will allow me to be silly, then?"

"If you must, but I sincerely hope these episodes are infrequent." I sounded annoyed even to my own ears, but I was still feeling a trifle resentful at having been pulled through a knothole over horses.

"Well, I am sorry to tell you, Mr. Darcy, that I am feeling silly over another matter altogether."

"We are not done wrangling?" I asked, as an overwhelming wave of feeling for this woman gripped me. What I would not do for her! "Tell me, then," I said, struggling not to push a stray curl off her forehead.

"You are unlikely to deposit my sister and me at Piccadilly Circus, sir." I knew exactly what road we were now on, and I steeled myself as she continued. "We shall traverse Cheapside, enter Gracechurch Street, and pull up to number twelve, the home of my uncle who is in trade—a place and situation to be deplored by everybody, according to Mr. Bingley's sisters."

"And—?"

"Your sister—"

"My sister will be perfectly amenable," I replied dryly, and then out of irritation, out of the unceasing harassment of wanting such a perverse, difficult, headstrong and beautiful woman, I put my fingers to her forehead as my mother did to me when I was a child. "Are you ill? I think you might have taken a chill this morning in Kent. That would explain this strange turn."

She chuckled but turned back to the window nonetheless, and so I came up behind her, as near as I dared, and spoke softly into her ear.

"I would wish you thought better of me, Elizabeth Bennet."

Unfortunately, we were in this lover-like attitude, this dangerous proximity, when Richard breezed in. Thankfully, he did not so much as raise an eyebrow as Elizabeth and I abruptly separated.

"Shall we go, Cousin?" he asked.

"Take Miss Elizabeth down, will you, Richard. I shall settle with Martin and be with you directly."

I stood in that room, wrung out and on fire.

When I was finally able to move, I went below and settled with the innkeeper before I stepped outside and into my waiting coach. Richard sat in an attitude of nonchalance, pretending to look out the window, and I tolerated his smirking for ten miles before my impatience boiled over.

"What is it?" I snapped.

"Nothing! The day is fine, is it not?"

"If you must have it, we had a row."

My cousin's façade of insouciance fell off. "Did I not tell you to behave better with Miss Elizabeth?"

"It could not be helped." Somehow that realization calmed me. "I may have even made progress," I confessed, sitting back and stretching out my legs. This was a tentative position, but something in that heated encounter had struck me as reciprocal.

"You looked to be making very good *progress* when I came in the room," Richard said with a chuckle.

"She is unnerved by my wealth."

"Is she? Unnerved you say?"

"Mm-hmm. Quite put off. Her uncle is a tradesman who lives in Cheapside, and I was making a show with a grand repast and my own teams."

"And did you reassure her?"

I smiled and told him I had while thinking my cousin would consider our brutal conference a strange way to reassure a lady.

"Enough of me," I said after a deep breath. "I thank you for tending to Miss Mary. I would not have had the chance to disabuse Miss Elizabeth of her notions otherwise."

Richard smiled. "You make Miss Mary sound like hard duty."

"All the better if you do not think she is."

He laughed and shook his head before he went back to watching the streams of farms and villages pass us by—dreaming of his property, no doubt. I then spoke to him of various thoughts I had had about where and how he should settle when he sold his commission, and we passed the time pleasurably. Only in the back of my mind did I entertain the nagging worry that I would not measure up upon presenting myself to Elizabeth's relations in trade.

Lord, do not let me betray so much as a twitch of dismay!

AT BROMLEY, ELIZABETH AND I CIRCLED EACH OTHER LIKE RIVAL dogs. We had both been bitten in Maidstone, and thirty miles later, we affected great politeness since neither of us would yield to the dominance of the other—fitting since a matched pair by definition presupposes equal points.

"What troubles you, William?" Georgiana asked.

We sat waiting for tea in a snug at the Green Goose. Elizabeth, Mary, and Mrs. Annesley were at the window looking at the church across the square, and Richard had gone to secure ale for the coachmen and grooms.

I could think of no subtle way to speak to my sister of my misgivings, so I spoke plainly. "We shall soon arrive at the home of Miss Elizabeth's uncle. He is in trade."

"Oh yes," she said. "Elizabeth and Mary have been telling me about the Gardiners. They sound very agreeable people. I wonder whether we might have Mrs. Gardiner to tea. I have told my friends to come tomorrow."

The anticipation of a jump that turns out to be nothing but a clump of grass will leave a person rather flat. "Of course you must invite her," I said stupidly.

Was I the only member of my party bracing for an unwelcome acquaintance? Apparently so. Richard, whose tours in Spain had brushed all the polish off of him, could mix with anybody. From the window, I saw him regaling his batman, Sergeant Brown, with something lewd from the sound of their laughter.

I had a dozen miles in which I prayed to be cured of my priggishness. Our progress into the city was naturally slow, and when we finally arrived at Gracechurch Street, I was immeasurably relieved to see Mr. Gardiner's house stood in a perfectly ordinary neighborhood removed from the principal bustle of the city. Briskly, Richard and I stepped out and helped the Bennet sisters down.

The townhouse door opened, and a pretty lady, younger than I expected, came down the steps.

"Lizzy! Mary! What is this?" she cried, but with a mixture of gracious welcome intermingled with her surprise.

"Oh, Aunt, you would not credit—but I must make you known to our new friend, Miss Georgiana Darcy."

Mrs. Gardiner went instantly to my sister and, after a graceful curtsey, said, "Miss Darcy? But you must be from Pemberley in Derbyshire. I grew up in Lambton, and I met your mother, oh, many times. How delightful to make your acquaintance! And how kind of you to take up my nieces. Will you not come in?"

"No no, Aunt. We have had a full day of travel and settled it that we shall go to Miss Darcy's for tea tomorrow if you will allow it."

"I hope you will come too, Mrs. Gardiner," Georgiana added shyly.

"Certainly, and very happy to do so. Where shall we go?"

I listened as my sister gave the lady my Mayfair address and then

Elizabeth said, "Mr. Darcy, Colonel Fitzwilliam, allow me to introduce my aunt Mrs. Gardiner—oh, and my uncle too, I see. Uncle Gardiner, you must come and meet my friends."

Could this be Mrs. Bennet's brother? I tried not to stare as a well-favored man, beaming of intelligence and sophistication, came down the stairs to stand next to his wife.

He kissed his nieces and spoke to Elizabeth. "Well, scamp, you have surely gotten into a scrape if you arrive like a package tossed out on the curb. What have you done, then?"

She laughed. "Oh, I assure you I was very bad, sir, and you had better scold me half the night. But first, may I introduce you to Mr. Darcy?"

Chapter 20

Elizabeth's Story...

I cannot describe the terror and the thrill of the danger in which I found myself while in London. Mr. Darcy, while never completely charming, strove for politeness with my family, and upon occasion, he exhibited a graciousness that turned my head. We had tea twice at his beautiful townhouse, went to an exhibition of paintings, and visited Hatchards. One might wonder why I would call these pleasant excursions a danger, but I had come to think of my aunt and uncle Gardiner as my last line of defense against Mr. Darcy's incursions into my heart. He was beginning to quite overpower my resistance.

The man's efforts to be agreeable to my relations instead pushed me further and further into irreversible admiration. Even my body betrayed me. My knees turned strangely weak upon seeing him, my heart raced, my cheeks flamed, and when he spoke, I held my breath like a halfwit.

Not even the harshest internal remonstrations could shake me out of my wilting sensibilities. When I looked over my half dozen dresses with a wave of dismay, I knew I was beyond redemption. To wish for comely dresses to catch a man's eye was my sister Lydia's most constant whine!

"What is amiss, Lizzy?" Aunt Gardiner asked when I arrived in the parlor before dinner in a dress that had been perfectly acceptable for dinner at Rosings Park but now felt like a potato sack.

"Oh, Aunt," I said, wishing I could laugh at myself, but somehow, those two words came gushing out in a sound resembling a sob. If that were not horrifying enough, when I looked into her kindly, affectionate face, tears clouded my vision and forced me to find the handkerchief I had tucked into the lace of my sleeve. "I cannot talk about it easily," I finally said, brushing the destruction of my face away with a watery smile.

My aunt did not smile back at me or cajole me. She looked at me very much as Mr. Bromley would, as though seeing inside my head and finding an alarming malformation.

"You do not need to talk about it," she said gently. "I have eyes."

How lowering! My cheeks flooded for the hundredth time that week, and I looked downward. "I begin to hate this dress," I said. There—I had laid out the whole of my distress in a form of code.

"Of course you do. I am sure the gentleman has seen it a dozen times already. No no, Lizzy. There is no escaping the sad fact that you would like to show yourself to advantage. You are not Mrs. Wollstonecraft, you know. You should not expect to be always invulnerable." She stood back and looked at me appraisingly with her dimples on full display. "A little humility would look well on you, my girl."

I could not help but grin sheepishly at her, and exercising the small store of humility I possessed, I thanked her for her forbearance.

She laughed aloud and discomposed me altogether when she said, "Think nothing of your dress. When Mr. Darcy looks at you with his heart rising in his eyes, he cannot notice what you are wearing."

This was the irritant I needed, and I sniffed back the last of my tears and stood two inches taller. "You will pardon me for wishing to arm myself. I would like to have a shield at least! Am I to be so easily felled that he can push me over like a rootless tree with his melting looks?"

"Come along, then," she said.

And though we came down ten minutes late and left my uncle to do the pretty with our guests, I swept down the stairs, equal to seeing Mr. Darcy in a hastily hemmed blue silk gown belonging to my aunt.

We sat down to dinner. Mr. Darcy accompanied his sister and Colonel Fitzwilliam, and my aunt had invited Mr. Bromley so that our numbers were even. We were a small party, and conscious of Miss Darcy not being out, we did not conduct ourselves with overbearing formality. In this, our soon-to-be brother helped us by playfully engaging Colonel Fitzwilliam's leading remarks or contributing light responses to my aunt's polished direction of the conversation.

Trying not to compare this convivial meal with the uproar of dinners at Longbourn, I began recovering my balance from my earlier nonsense over a dress—and had just made my uncle laugh aloud by telling him of Mr. Collins's terror of his pigs—when I found myself thrown into confusion once again.

"Where do you go after your wedding, Mr. Bromley?" Mr. Darcy asked.

"We travel to Berkshire to visit my father. He is settled comfortably in Reading, but his bursitis does not allow him to come to us."

Mr. Darcy then asked in the style of a chatterbox, "Will you take your family to Miss Bennet's wedding, Mrs. Gardiner?"

"Just my husband and I shall go. Mr. Gardiner and I had planned to take a tour of the Lakes this summer but amended our plans for the happy occasion of Jane's wedding. Instead, we shall go straight from Meryton to visit my family, and we hope to take Lizzy and Mary with us."

Since this was news to me, I looked up at her in surprise as did my sister. My aunt casually assured us we could decide our willingness to go at our leisure.

Miss Darcy also sat up at this news. "But your family is in Lambton, is it not?"

"Why, yes. My grandfather had the bookshop there, and my father was curate before he died. I have a few aunts remaining and cousins and friends too that I have wanted to visit, and there are many beauty spots I recall from my girlhood that I hope to see."

"You were Mr. Parker's daughter then?" Mr. Darcy asked.

"Do you remember him, sir? I believe you were often at school, but your parents were very kind to him and came to tea once when my mother was still living."

"I remember him very well, ma'am. But if you are so close to Pemberley, you must stay with us. The inn at Lambton is not in the best repair, and my sister and I would be delighted to have you." He glanced at Miss Darcy and received a look of shy encouragement. "And if you enjoy fishing," he said, turning to my uncle, "summers are ideal for lake trout."

"You tempt me, sir," Uncle Gardiner replied with a look of pleasure, and nothing more was said to the purpose until after dinner when we were seated together in the parlor.

Miss Darcy came to me. "Pray, say you will convince your aunt to let you stay at Pemberley." I glanced uncertainly at Aunt Gardiner, who stood with my uncle and Mr. Darcy in animated conversation.

Thinking to see what sense Mary made of this mad plan, I looked for her. She was speaking with Colonel Fitzwilliam, and from what I could infer, he was telling her of the pleasures of Mr. Darcy's park in summer.

I smiled wanly at Georgiana and struggled with a growing sense of unease. That Mr. Darcy nurtured a tendre for me, even my aunt now openly acknowledged. But how could he offer me more than his admiration? I thought of his estate, a place that could stable fifty horses, described by his cousin as a kind of Elysium. Had not Miss Bingley waxed poetically about his palatial house and the enormity of his collection of silver? Inwardly, I quailed. This was too much!

Just when I had resolved to be ill or to batten myself on my newly married sister Jane—anything that would rescue me from going to Pemberley and facing my multiple inadequacies—Mr. Darcy and my aunt approached.

He peered at me and said, "Mrs. Gardiner, might I have a few minutes with your niece outside and in plain view of that window?"

As he helped me to stand and walked me toward the door, I heard Mary say in a confidential tone, "Do not worry, Aunt. Mr. Darcy also had to talk sense into Lizzy at Hunsford when she was determined we should take the mail coach."

Mr. Darcy's Story...

"I SEE YOU ARE HAVING ANOTHER ATTACK OF LUNACY AND MEAN TO refuse my invitation if you can," I said sternly. "What is it now? Does my house have too many rooms? Is my park too large to suit you?"

Elizabeth and I stood face-to-face as though on a stage, lit by the lamps of the parlor and framed in the rectangle of Mrs. Gardiner's front window. To my absolute horror, a few tears spilled over and down her cheeks.

Rather than crumble while weeping, as Georgiana would, she stood taller, and those looking at us would not think anything amiss since our faces were covered by the gathering dark.

"You have bested me, Mr. Darcy," she said in a small, plain voice.

"I had not thought we were fighting for once," I said, almost desperate to understand her. "We have said many honest things to one another, Elizabeth Bennet. You must now simply say what has upset you, for I have not the lights to pick apart your very complicated objections to staying at Pemberley."

She swallowed and looked at me, imploring me not to be stupid. But upon seeing my growing bewilderment, she said with the briskness of a woman forced to say what she would rather not, "Do you not see? I have fallen in love with you, Mr. Darcy, and things being unequal as they are, it would be kind of you to find an excuse for our not accepting your invitation."

By some miracle, I did not fall backward as though I had been hit in the jaw. Instead, I came to full attention at the way she stood before me as though she meant to refuse me before I had the chance to offer for her.

"My lord!" I barked. "What are you? A fiend? You have led me here to this spot on earth—pushing, pulling, and utterly bewitching me with your every breath—and *now* you stand there wringing your handkerchief and crying quits?"

She stood quite still, which was just as well because I was nowhere near finished speaking. "What next? Will you now tell me that your position would pull me down, that out of kindness for my consequence—a thing you have always hated—you must sadly decline to know me? You—you," I stuttered, "you mean to point out the unhappy fact that my relations will object to the connection, that my sister deserves someone who can bring her out in society, and that you are unequal to being mistress of anything grander than a clumsy cottage with a kitchen garden!"

"Mr. Darcy, you are raising your voice."

"Of course I am!" I roared. "I am at my wit's end, Elizabeth. You have driven me stark raving mad. Can you not see that I adore you? That I would do anything for you?"

She then bowed her head and discretely made use of her handkerchief. "You have never said so."

"And when would I have done so? You have anticipated me! I had the thing planned very well, I assure you," I said with less rage and more petulance. My romantic notions of bended knee in Pemberley wood and my mother's ring in my pocket were in shards all around me.

Then, seeing that my heart was battered as she stood before me, I said in a far gentler tone, "There are no obstacles, my love. I am a gentleman, and you are a gentleman's daughter. We belong to one another, and I mean to have you, even if I must pull you aside and shout at you a hundred times over."

She again took refuge in her handkerchief, and glancing at the window, I passed her mine. "You had better make quick work of recovering your composure, Elizabeth, because we have treated our relations to a scene. I believe your uncle comes to rescue you."

True enough, Mr. Gardiner appeared in that small patch of light where we stood in the front garden off of Gracechurch Street. "Well, Lizzy? I have come to see whether there are any bloody wounds in need of stitching."

"Sir, I mean your niece no harm," I protested.

The man laughed gently. "Of course you do not, Mr. Darcy. I came to see whether *you* were still intact. By the looks of it, you have taken several hard blows. Will you come to see me at my office in the morning? Meanwhile, your sister has said she wishes to go home. Goodnight, Mr. Darcy."

I turned to see Richard and Georgiana peering at me from the stoop, and trying not to stumble, I left to join them.

Chapter 21

Elizabeth's Story...

"He is horrible," I sniffed.

"Yes, yes," Uncle Gardiner said. We sat alone in the parlor on the sofa, a single lamp burning low. He put his arm around me, and clutching Mr. Darcy's handkerchief, I cuddled deep into his shoulder.

"Mr. Darcy will not let you come over the top of him, and you do not like that one bit."

"No! And he is arrogant," I said, sniffling just the once. "You should have seen the way he looked at Mama."

"I can only imagine," my uncle said dryly.

"He was very severe when he visited Papa."

"Was he? Well, in that I must hold him blameless. Who would not be severe when trying to get Mr. Bennet to talk seriously about anything?"

I made a grumbling sound. The rhythmic tick of the clock seemed to drown out the vague sounds of the city at night as I sat up in protest. "He is obscenely rich, Uncle!"

He pulled me down to his shoulder and humbly admitted that I was perfectly right to object to a fortune. And after I could think of no more objections he said, "I shall speak to him tomorrow, Lizzy."

"What will you say to him?"

"That he must either offer for you or leave you alone, my girl. We cannot have any more of these alarums. Your sister is to marry, I have a business to run, and your aunt has a family to raise. If you must be the center of a contretemps, then I suggest you run away to Drury Lane because we are too busy to attend to you." He softened this harsh statement with a kiss to my forehead. "What is it to be then?"

"I love him, Uncle."

"I know you do. The thing is not so very hard to figure out, is it?"

"He will have to go to Longbourn," I said mournfully.

"If he loves you, he will bear the mortification. And, if you love him, you will suffer through the humiliation. Make your decision, and either marry the poor man or let him go. You have thoroughly done him in."

"Have I?" I asked, suddenly feeling a little heartier and sitting up.

My uncle chuckled. "He was reeling, child. You have staggered a great man."

"Well," I said, blowing my nose, "he deserves it. He has caused me to weep in public."

"Terrible. So, will you make him pay for it by marrying him?" I fell back on his shoulder and nodded.

"Good. I shall speak to him in the morning and tell him to collect you for a drive in the park if the weather holds fine. If not, he can speak to you here. Now, let me up. I must dig around the attics and see if my fishing pole is intact. I hope to be spared from half your aunt's visits on the excuse of angling."

After he left me, my aunt put me to bed as though I suffered from consumption, and Mary came with her candle to kiss me goodnight. My lord, what a terrific loss of composure I had suffered! No wonder everyone treated me like a physical wreck.

The morning broke fine, but I was still on the list of those of *uncertain temper*, or so it seemed. Mary brought me a cup of tea, and my aunt breezed in with one of her summer muslins for me to try on.

Looking upon my sister's smile of pity and my aunt's forced cheerfulness, I sat up and said mournfully, "I am so embarrassed."

"As you should be," Aunt Gardiner said lightly. "Mr. Bromley discretely offered to mix you a composer. But never mind that. We must do what we can to stitch up your courage because I expect Mr. Darcy as soon as may be, and you will treat him with a little deference for once, Lizzy."

"I like him very well," Mary put forward tentatively, as though trying to convince me.

"I like him too," I protested, "but I did not account for how hard it would be to sacrifice my independence. And to give it up to such an imperious man," I added with a frown.

Good God. He would direct everything!

My sister looked at me in confusion. "But you will be the most independent woman I know," she said.

"Will I? Will I, Aunt?"

She laughed at me and sat on the bed. "You will be privileged and have things just as you like them. Mr. Darcy does not do anything by halves."

I fell back on my pillow in dawning comprehension. They were right.

"No, he does not do anything in half measures. He will have *me*, after all, and I am a whole world of perturbation."

"Just so," she said, delightedly clapping her hands. "You must stand upon that foundation and come down to breakfast. And then we shall plan out our excursion to Derbyshire."

My aunt's pale-peach sprigged muslin dotted with tiny white flowers, once hemmed for my height, was the perfect antidote to my mortification. The French cut flattered my frame and featured a ruche at the high waist of the gown that flared out the back in a most satisfying swirl when I walked. I found Mary in the nursery, and together we went down to the parlor.

"Would you like to practice?" she asked.

"I would rather hear you play the Mozart," I said, picking up my book from the table by the window. That window would, for some time to come, cause me to think upon Mr. Darcy, and so I put the book down and listened to Mary. When a black perch phaeton with matching horses pulled in front of the house, I stood and went to where my aunt was busy writing at a little table.

"I shall go out and spare him the trial of small talk."

"Yes, Lizzy. Do go, and I shall see you when you return," she said, putting her hand on my cheek.

Mr. Darcy's Story...

ELIZABETH MET ME AT THE DOOR AS I WAS RAISING MY HAND TO THE knocker. She smiled tentatively and searched my face. I gravely took her hand, led her down the walk, and without saying a word, handed her up to the bench. The tiger let go the horses, and as we trotted forward, he jumped on the back.

"Where would you like to go?" I asked to break the silence between us.

"Anywhere you would like to take me," she replied.

"Docility is it?"

"I mean to be amiable today. Shall we talk of Ritter, sir?"

I had spent eighteen sober hours barely strung together, and my short laugh sounded rusty to my ears. I looked over at Elizabeth, and when she offered me a modest smile ripe with both apology and trepidation, I reciprocated in kind.

"All will be well, my heart," I said.

"Will it, Mr. Darcy?"

"I shall make it so," I said, and then, traffic being heavy, I worked the team and we lapsed into our private reflections. The day was not the finest, but it was passably warm with clouds drifting overhead softening the light to a diffuse glow. We came briskly into the park, and I tooled us over the well-traveled avenues toward the Serpentine. The fashionable hour had not yet come, and once we had gone over the bridge, the number of visitors dwindled to an occasional person seeking solitude or a party of young men partaking of brisk exercise.

I pulled to a wide spot on the road, handed the ribbons to my tiger—a ready specimen twelve years of age who called me 'Gov'— and took Elizabeth to a bench screened by willows overlooking the water. A few of Queen Charlotte's swans floated past, and I searched for some means of opening the most pivotal conversation of my life.

As though she sensed my agitation, Elizabeth reached for my hand, and I knew then that all *would* be well. Instead of some grand speech, I simply confessed to her.

"I shall not say this well, you know. I have the unhappy knack of sounding like a bumptious prig whenever I want to impress you."

"That is one of the reasons I have come to love you, Mr. Darcy," she said in the gentlest voice I have yet heard. "Shall we marry, then?"

She had just spared me the exercise, and I took the back of her hand to my lips. "As soon as may be if you are feeling stout."

"You overwhelm me," she said in her smallest voice.

"And you terrify me," I replied bluntly, pulling forth that reluctant smile.

"You are very grand, sir."

My turn had come to smile. "And you are very pert, miss."

This earned me a chuckle, but when she seemed to be caught by the sight of a scull with two rowers gliding past us, she did not speak again.

"I adore you, Elizabeth."

"I am lost to you, Mr. Darcy," she replied, still looking at the skull but with her cheeks warmed.

"I dream of you most nights."

She finally turned to look at me. "And I think of you every day."

Again, we floundered.

"Might we walk, sir?" she asked, standing.

And so we meandered down the lane, our hands refusing to release one another, and after a moment, Elizabeth came out of her abstracted state.

"One cannot wonder that lovers want to be private."

"Do you refer to our singularly stupid conversation, my love?"

"My head is both full and empty at the same time. I have nothing clever or charming with which to tease you."

"And I have nothing whatsoever dashing to say. I do hope I recover my wits eventually. I have never spoken so much sentiment."

"I am a little partial to sentiment."

"Really! Well, I shall brush up on it then."

"Was my uncle very harsh this morning?"

"Hardly. He informed me I had better marry you or leave you alone. I handed him the settlements to look over and told him in my most officious tone that he would have a terrible time ridding himself of me because I meant to have you, come what may. We then fell to talk of fishing, and for the sake of form, because I could hardly call on you an hour early, he gave me a tour of his warehouses, and we talked of his business."

"Might we—might I ask after your family, sir?"

I stopped in the middle of the path and turned to face her. "Elizabeth Bennet, you may say anything to me, anytime you wish to say it. Even if you enrage me, I prefer to know what you are thinking to having you mince around me as though you are addressing a fragile prince. What is it you want to know?"

"What will your uncle say?"

"The earl will fail to recognize me at his club."

"One thing I admire most about you is that you are willing to tell me the unvarnished truth," she said. "And your aunt the countess?"

"You may expect the cut direct if we should meet on Bond Street."

"Lady Catherine?"

"Oh, she is another matter entire. She will want to have a warrant posted for your arrest so that she can see you hung by the neck at the gates of Rosings Park."

We began walking again. "Colonel Fitzwilliam?"

"Supportive."

"His brother?"

"Langford? In public, he will snub us because my uncle determines his allowance and he will need to march in step with Matlock's opinions. In private, he cannot be brought to care about anything except his dissipations."

"Your sister?"

"In alt. She hopes to have you for a sister and, as a side benefit, longs to be overlooked when she makes her dreaded debut."

"Truly?"

"I never told you, Elizabeth, but Wickham insinuated himself in her society when Georgiana was on holiday and convinced her to elope with him. She fancied herself in love, and only by chance did I arrive in time to rout him. My sister has since worried she cannot distinguish between a man who loves *her* and a man who loves her inheritance."

"You shock me. No wonder the mention of his name—"

"At Netherfield, yes. I could not continue our flirtation on account of the urge to go and strangle that man."

"But your sister! Now I understand why you kept silent with regard to his lies."

"Until I was told to do otherwise, yes. But that was only the first time you chastened me. I did not know then that you would do so again and again." Inwardly, I braced myself for a lifetime of being sent to the right-about by this diminutive spark at my side.

"I have not been as bad as that."

"Not bad? You have caused me, Fitzwilliam Darcy, a man of sense and dignity, to lose my temper, my composure, and my bearings, and that is not all. You have harassed me into such a disordered state that

I resorted to publicly shouting hyperbole at you in full view of a party of our relations. You, Elizabeth Bennet, have been positively wicked."

"My uncle says I staggered a great man," she put forth with an impish smile.

I laughed, pulled her close, and with my arm around her, I stumbled us forward like a drunk with his barmaid.

"That you have, my love."

We came laughing to a small sliver of shingle and stood there as the water lapped at the stones. All our merriment subsided, and we looked at one another with wonder.

"What next, Mr. Darcy?" she whispered, her eyes glinting like jewels.

"You are about to be kissed, madam," I said, and then I made good my threat.

Chapter 22

Dearest Papa,

Mr. Darcy plans to visit you on Friday, and I hope you will at least be civil. Do just what he says, sir, and I shall absolve you of every arrears of parenting of which you stand accused.

Your loving daughter,
Lizzy

Elizabeth's Story...

That evening, I took my note to my uncle's post tray and then went to the front parlor. There I sat by the window and looked out, unseeing.

My vision was perpetually turned inward in the days following my betrothal, and I craved solitude in order to review my most recent conversations with Mr. Darcy.

"When did you fall in love with me, sir?" I had asked him only the day before in a low voice as we huddled in the dim back row of the atlases at Hatchards. Our sisters were looking at the illustrated histories on the lower floor, and my aunt was herding two of my young cousins around in search of books to read to them.

He pulled me deeper into the shadows and then held out his two hands as though catching rain. "My fate was sealed by increments, rather like coins on a scale—the first being dropped when you warned me against dancing with you a second time." His left hand lowered an inch and his right hand compensated equally upward. "I had never danced twice with anybody for fear of being caught, you know."

"I see. I stole your trick. And then?"

"Then I saw your ankle." He smiled rakishly as his left hand moved theatrically downward and his right hand went further up, and he repeated this motion with each successive point. "You were afraid of my horse. You marched down Oakham Mount like a foot soldier. You teased me about having learnt your ABCs, and you flounced away— while limping—after I enraged you at a ball."

"You have the strangest notions of comely behavior."

"But you have never seen how comely you appear in full retreat, my girl."

"Are there any more coins you wish to report?" I asked, waving at his imaginary scale.

"You looked so fragile with your foot on a stool the next day when I came to tell your father about Wickham. And you had two of everything to eat at Maidenstone. The fashion of elegant starvation has never appealed to me."

"No? Miss Bingley seems to have mastered the art. I never saw anyone take more bites from a square inch of beef in my life."

"A woman who does not eat is prone to fainting," he said with asperity.

"I can safely promise I shall never faint from hunger, sir."

"Good. And now, may I move my arms? I am beginning to feel a strain in my shoulders."

"That is because you are a fragile prince," I said. "But hold there. Suppose when we are married, I fall into the sullens and snipe at you.

What of your famous scale then?"

The left hand came up a fraction. "I believe that would be the worst of it."

I scoffed at his optimism. "And if I lost this tooth here?" I pointed to my right front incisor.

He dropped his hands. "Truly, Elizabeth? You wish me to anticipate such an eventuality?"

I put his hands back into their scale positions. "I stand before you with a large gap in my smile. Oh, and I have opted to wear a matronly cap to cover a gray streak on my head."

He dropped his hands, looked about, took my face in his hands and kissed me in a public place.

"Mr. Darcy!" I huffed, my face aflame.

He spoke hotly into my ear. "Do you think your missing tooth and your gray hair could put me off? I mean to show you the meaning of devotion."

A short gentleman in a red waistcoat appeared around the row, and we broke apart, pretending to look earnestly at the spines of the books in front of us. Mr. Darcy then leaned over and whispered, "You know, we could have a gold tooth fashioned for you."

"I suppose." I whispered back.

"Very well. Have we settled that I shall always love you?"

"Yes, I suppose," I said with flippant disregard, though I confess my heart was pounding with a strong passion for him.

"Now, since you have rushed me into this understanding, I am forced to give you this trinket to seal our bargain. When we go to Pemberley, you may have your choice from my mother's jewel box or something new if you prefer."

I realized with a start that Mr. Darcy, the most imposing man I had ever met, was in a state of insecurity over his token. He confirmed this by muttering, "This was the smallest, most inconsequential thing I could see in the case, and not wanting to enrage you with my notions of a suitable—"

"But that is beautiful!" I cried, immediately stifling my outburst with my gloved hand.

Mr. Darcy looked at me uncertainly before he beamed out a smile of triumph. His expression of relief stayed with me still as I sat there at the window of my uncle's Cheapside house. I gazed lovingly down at my finger. There sat a startlingly large ruby bound on all sides by tiny pearls set on a band far too large, and my heart burst for the hundredth time. Nothing about his ring suited either my size or my taste for understatement, but I sat enthralled, for in this small object, Mr. Darcy rested his promise to me.

"You had better become accustomed to owning jewels, Lizzy," Aunt Gardiner said crisply, having come upon me gazing fondly at my ring. "Are you ready?"

"Ready?"

"We go to the dressmaker today. My goodness! I have told you three times this morning that you have a fitting."

"Mr. Darcy goes to Hertfordshire today," I said as though this explained my stupidity.

"Yes, Lizzy," Mary said crossly, coming up behind my aunt. "The entire house has heard this news. Put on your bonnet for goodness sake."

And so we went. My aunt, anticipating the need for my trousseau, had the forethought to take me to her French dressmaker to be measured and to select patterns, fabrics, and the like. "You will need a significant wardrobe," she said ominously.

Not merely *suitable*—significant. My father would be expected to send what funds he could spare to the purpose, and if he did not, my aunt assured me she would pay for all in expectation of repayment when I got my pin money.

When I looked nonplussed at the idea of pin money, she pursed her lips and could not be made to say what she knew. I was aware

Mr. Darcy had talked of my settlement with my uncle, and not wanting to feel daunted by the wonder of my impending fortune, I subsided into meek submission to all her plans.

After half an hour of looking at the most sumptuous fabrics I had ever seen in my life, I said, "Aunt, how much may I spend, do you think?"

She raised both eyebrows and primly said, "You can certainly afford that silk."

"Can I bespeak fabric for my sisters?"

"Safely, my love."

"And for you?"

"If you wish, but you know you need not give me a thing. You have entertained me very well these last few weeks."

"Mary, come to me," I said. Thus, I eased into the notion of having a dressmaker of the highest standards selecting three fabrics that did justice to Mary's subtle coloring and bespeaking for her a morning gown, a new travelling dress, and a ball gown.

"Lizzy, you are shockingly intemperate. For what do I need such finery?" she protested.

"You will come to Pemberley, for one thing, and for another, if I must dress like a peacock, then I wish not to be alone in my plumage. Does Colonel Fitzwilliam like blue, do you think?"

"He is in Surrey as well you know," she said tartly. She did not like me pressing on this sore spot, for she fostered a hopeless tendre for the dashing colonel.

"But he will get leave to return for the wedding."

"Very well, but I favor the green."

"For my wedding? You wish to tell the world you envy me?"

She smiled at last. "I do envy you, Lizzy."

"Green it is, then."

We lingered over the fabrics, selecting bolts of yellow for Lydia, pink for Kitty, sky blue for Jane, and gold for Mama. My aunt, when pressed, confessed to a preference for dotted ivory jacquard, and for an hour altogether I did not once worry about how Mr. Darcy fared at Longbourn.

While standing on a stool being measured, however, the idea of my mother's fit of raptures, of the shocking things she would say to Mr. Darcy about catching husbands for Kitty and Lydia, did once or twice intrude upon my serenity. Thinking to dampen my rising anxiety from further imagining what shrieking would ensue from my sisters at the notion of my marrying before them, I cajoled my aunt into looking for hats, shoes, and all manner of items to go with my significant wardrobe.

She assured me I could well afford whatever luxuries I chose, and I plowed ahead, perfectly dazzled, considering that only a fortnight prior, I sat on a trunk in a well-worn wool gown outside my cousin's rectory. When I selected three shawls of silk, Indian paisley, and cashmere, Mary began to pucker up, and wishing to avoid her conversion back to pious scold, I tamely put the silk back on the shelf and pronounced my efforts at a stand.

We ended our excursion at a teashop, and by the time we arrived back in Cheapside from Bond Street, I fell onto my bed for a much-needed nap. This was just as well because the night passed with restless anxiety over Mr. Darcy's exposure to my family, and only by recalling in minute detail the many horrible moments I had spent with *his* family in Kent, did I find any peace at all.

Chapter 23

Mr. Darcy's Story...

My great-grandfather purchased a famous painting of William the Conqueror, sword raised in triumph, during the battle of Hastings. It hangs in the formal entryway at Pemberley. I thought of the painting with the trace of a smile as I made my way in stately haste from Meryton back to London. The settlement papers were tucked securely in a case beside me, and I had in my pocket three dates given to me by the rector of Elizabeth's parish. The first banns would be read on Sunday, and my nerves thrummed steadily, certain I had made a magnificent choice of a bride.

In the morning, I whistled as Carsten and I went through the ritual of dressing.

"You are in spirits today, sir," he said.

"I am. Have my tailor visit me, will you?"

This would alert the entire house that I was on the verge of something. That I went willingly to Cheapside every day since my return from Kent must have sparked a few wild theories at least, but my tailor coming would tell all. From the butler to the lowliest kitchen maid, the whole house would come to the correct conclusion in the space of five seconds, for I had not made any attempt whatsoever to disguise my interest in my sister's new acquaintance when she came for tea.

When I was turned out, I went to the music room. I stood in the doorway while Georgiana finished her piece before I asked Mrs. Annesley for a moment with my sister.

I took Georgiana to the library and said, "You had better congratulate me."

"Have you done it? William, have you?"

"You may fully expect to have your Season cut in half. Lady Matlock will know soon enough. Do not fool yourself that there will be no unpleasantness."

"But I am equal to anything now." She took my hands and cried out with pure joy. "Let them gnash their teeth at me."

"Brave talk, nursling. I am going to Cheapside." What a happy sentence that had turned out to be. "Will you come?"

Mr. and Mrs. Gardiner made everything effortless for me. Elizabeth, a picture of demure womanhood, sat at a table on the far side of the room, pretending to do needlework, and after a few tidy greetings, I found myself ushered over to take my tea with her. Meanwhile, Mrs. Gardiner took Mary and Georgiana into a deep conference over a periodical, and I saw that Elizabeth's uncle meant to read his newspaper.

This afforded me sufficient privacy to look warmly into my love's eyes and say, "Well, fiend? How have you fared?"

"Was it awful?" she asked, her eyes alight.

"Dreadful. But simple enough."

"Simple? Papa did not give you fits and starts?"

"He did not have the opportunity to do so."

"How can that be? He knew you were coming. I wrote to him." She looked puzzled. "I expected him to pretend not to understand you for a quarter of an hour or to claim he had promised me to a tenant farmer or some such."

"He may have wished to quiz me, but I did not relish the prospect. And so I went first to wait on your mother."

"Mama? You went to wait on her?"

"Mm-hmm," I said with enraging casualness. "I told her—quietly, I should add, as your sisters were visiting your Aunt Philips and I found her alone for once—that I had come to see Mr. Bennet about marrying her second daughter."

She laughed aloud, the sound straining the capacity of the other occupants of the room to ignore us but settling me into a sort of quiet joy. I could live my life on the sustaining sound of Elizabeth Bennet's laugh.

"You are a devil, Mr. Darcy," she said, subsiding back to a quiet murmur appropriate to our conference.

"Your father had less than five minutes with which to raise his brows at me and to hem and haw before Mrs. Bennet burst into the room and demanded he sign whatever I brought to be signed."

"Was she very loud?"

"Deafening. She sent a child at a run to collect your sisters, ordered up a punch with which to toast me, dragged your sister Jane down the stairs as well as the servants up the stairs, and even detained the post boy, who happened by at the wrong moment."

Elizabeth clasped her forehead, so I said, "I did passably well, I thought. After half an hour of it, I took your mother's hand, kissed her cheek, and pleaded the need for haste to return to my many affairs in London."

"You kissed my mother?"

"You will own the genius of it. She stood mute for half a minute, which enabled me to get away. But here," I said, pulling from my pocket the dates I had held so close. "Reverend Wharton says any of these will do."

"We shall marry before Jane!" she gasped.

"Your mother did not demure, nor did your sister. She looked surprised but willing to be happy. You have written to her?"

"Yes, yes. But so soon?"

"I am used to getting what I want when I want it, you know. I hope to be bumptious and carry you off with arrogant determination."

"To Pemberley?"

"I thought perhaps we could go on a tour of the lower counties. Would you like to go to the seashore? Anywhere you like, so long as we are in sufficient proximity to return for your sister's wedding. From there, we shall go to Pemberley with the Gardiners and anyone you would like to bring. I was hoping Mary would agree to go with us because she and Georgiana get on very well. In any case, I am amenable to your wishes. Think on it and tell me so that I can make arrangements."

Chapter 24

Elizabeth's Story…

Did Mr. Darcy and I march along in perfect harmony thereafter? No. That he insisted upon *arranging everything* caused me not infrequent bursts of consternation. And though I bravely acquiesced to most all his plans, twice I balked, requiring that the man pull me aside to try to speak sense to me.

Having settled it that we would marry on the third Sunday of May, that I would go next week to Hertfordshire in his coach and four with my sister, a maid, a coachman, a groom, and a footman, and that after our wedding we would travel in the grand style of sultan and sultana on a tour of the south downs and its storied cliffs, I felt I had surrendered quite enough. However, Mr. Darcy thought that aught was lacking upon hearing my faintest, most inconsequential anxiety that my wedding clothes might not all be ready to take home with me, he took my aunt aside.

The next morning brought him to our door, and after greeting me, he said, "You will excuse me this morning, I hope, Elizabeth. Mrs. Gardiner and I have an errand that should not take more than half an hour."

"An errand?" I asked in sudden suspicion.

He looked about, slightly guilty in my estimation. "I thought to see your dressmaker and assure that your things are ready when you leave Wednesday."

"You mean to pay her an exorbitant fee in order to assure it is so," I said grimly. In a trice, we faced each other outside, on the stoop this time since there fell off and on a drizzle of rain. "I forbid you to buy a priority on the making of my wedding clothes, Mr. Darcy."

"Well..." he said, striving for a reasonable note.

My resolution hardened. "No, not well. Not well at all."

"Your aunt thinks it a reasonable precaution, Elizabeth. She has advised me that, with the press of the Season, your dressmaker has not progressed to her satisfaction."

"You have enlisted her to your cause, have you? At what point, if any, was I to be consulted? Am I to be gainsaid on everything? In this I wish to have my way. If you bustle to her shop and hand her a fat package, then what other ladies will have their things put off? Why do you suppose *my* trousseau has not yet appeared ready to wear? What great lady has demanded she must have her opera gown overnight? What poor girl who does not have a Mr. Darcy to arrive on his white charger will face some meeting with her beau or her new relations in a borrowed dress in consequence?"

"I-I had not thought—"

"No. How could you? You have lived all your life this way. The merest wish of yours is the command of an army. But I refuse to be habituated in this way! We shall take our place in line, sir, unless the matter is one of grave importance. And I assure you, my dresses are not the stuff of life and death."

I watched in fascination as he struggled to digest my stern new ruling. After a moment, he managed a reluctant smile, let out a huff, and his shoulders fell by an inch.

"Will it always be thus between us, Elizabeth?"

"Do you mean shall we always debate our conflicts? I certainly hope so. I hope that I am not as easily mowed down as everyone else in your life has been. I hope as well that *some*, at least, of our contests I shall win."

"Very well. You have won this one. Might we at least go and see what *madame* has made ready for you? Afterward, there is something I would like to show you if you will give me your afternoon."

We did indeed go to my dressmaker, and upon recognizing the name 'Darcy,' the woman promised to redouble her efforts, which depressingly lessened my victory. However, the goodwill between Mr. Darcy and me was subsequently restored when he took me to the mews just this side of Richmond, and with a tenderness I had never seen in him, he showed me a newborn foal.

"She is to be Georgiana's birthday gift," he said softly, enumerating the little animal's lineage as though I knew all about her dame and sire and from whence they came. We spoke of his sister with all the affection we felt for her and marveled at the compelling sweetness of a newborn creature.

As Mr. Darcy handed me back into the landaulet, he said, "My love, you will never be ruined by good fortune, you know."

Ah, he had touched on the thorn directly. "I am afraid in the space of one week you will turn me into the most inflexible, tyrannical and overindulged woman ever born." He took my hand, and I said with great resolution, "And that is what I do not want to be."

"No, my heart. I shall endeavor to lower my expectations in all cases. But you will own that, having had things delivered to me on a silver salver for the whole of my life, my education will require your patience. My motives, I believe, are solid, for I only ever want to make you happy. But the means, I shall admit, require some adjustment. Now, come down off your pins, will you? You have won the day and should be lording your victory over me."

A few golden days passed before I once again had to remonstrate with my lover. I was to go home to help Mama with her frenetic wedding plans, and Mr. Darcy would finish his obligations in town before abandoning the metropolis for a prolonged stay at Pemberley. We anticipated our separation by spending a great deal of time sitting next to one another. Rarely was a dinner eaten when we were not at his house or he at my uncle's.

But on the very night before I was to go away, Mr. Darcy shook me once again into a state of high agitation. We were a very small party—my aunt and uncle, Mr. Darcy, and me. Both Mary and Georgiana had trifling colds and did not join us.

"I had meant to ask whether you have firmly settled on going to the coast for your wedding trip, Mr. Darcy," Aunt Gardiner asked as the dessert course came out.

Aware that our marriage notice would cause a stir and wishing to protect our happiest day from unpleasantness, we had determined we would be as far from society as possible: walking the cliff tops and admiring the waves out of reach of the gossips. Mr. Darcy explained this to my aunt, and then, as I remained in a delicious daydream of tasting salt air and holding my bonnet on my head in a stiff coastal wind, they continued to talk of particulars.

"I am nearly there, sir," Mr. Darcy had said.

Pleasantly I smiled and asked, "Nearly *where*? Am I allowed to know?"

"I am buying Netherfield Park," he said in the most passing manner! He turned to my uncle and, sipping from his glass of wine, continued. "Bingley's agent is slower than I would like, but all things considered, the deal is agreed upon. We wait only for the papers to be drawn up."

Mr. Darcy must have then taken a look at my face since his assured explanation dwindled into an expression of wary cautiousness. He applied his napkin to his lips, looked apologetically at my relations, and said, "I believe I have made a gross error. Might I make use of that patch of light in the front garden, ma'am?"

"Netherfield Park!" I cried. "Up against the small matter of my wedding clothes, this is monstrous!"

"Let me explain—"

"Let you? By all means, account for yourself!"

"I should have consulted you, Elizabeth. Will you excuse me just this once?"

"You may consult with me *now*, sir."

"Will you listen to me at least?"

"I shall try."

He took my hand and fidgeted with my ring. "I am to go to Hertfordshire to marry the woman of my dreams. My sister, her companion, and my cousin will come. We shall have with us my valet, two maids, and the giant."

"Your cousin's batman."

"Yes. And, your aunt and uncle come too, as well as Mr. Bromley, who has made plans to see us married and stay until his wedding to your sister. Upon that occasion, he will have with him two cousins and three of his close friends, one of them married."

"Yes, yes," I waved impatiently.

"Where at Longbourn would your mother put sixteen additional bodies?"

"There is an inn."

"There may very well be, Elizabeth, but if that establishment can offer more than ten beds, I would be surprised."

Assuming an expression of earnest innocence that did little to disguise the mischief in his eyes, he continued. "Besides, your mother will need a place to live if your father predeceases her. We cannot allow her to make a nest in the hedgerows." Before I could reply to that plum, he added, "And we shall necessarily visit your family from time to time. Would you not be more comfortable as mistress of your own house when you are in Hertfordshire?"

He had me at a disadvantage there, but the outlandish capacity to simply buy an estate for the sake of convenience had left me too shaken to acquiesce unresisting.

"The windows leak," I grumbled.

He listened to me with a grave expression and nodded soberly. "The land, however, yields well, and with better management, we could bring a few more people onto the estate."

"I can hardly step into that house without thinking of Caroline Bingley."

As though comforting a simpleton, Mr. Darcy gently took my hand and told me with his eyes that I was worth ten Caroline Bingleys.

"If there are five books in the library, I would be surprised."

Mr. Darcy removed my glove and took my hand to his lips and kissed it so, well, *explicitly,* I could hardly continue my objections. Soon we had stepped out of the patch of light, and he began kissing me elsewhere until I was so addled that, when we finally broke apart in a breathless passion, the purchase of Netherfield Park was a mere trifling.

When I could finally speak, I tried to sound more gracious than I felt after such a flaming defeat. "If my aunt and uncle stay at Netherfield, then I do not see why they could not bring their children, do you? When they go to Pemberley, my cousins can stay with Mama and enjoy a holiday of their own."

"I should have spoken to you, Elizabeth. I shall not be so highhanded in future."

"I did not know the Framingtons were willing to let the place go."

"They have not lived there for more than a decade. When my agent suggested a sale, the idea struck them as fortuitous."

"Mr. Bingley willingly gave up his right of first refusal, then?"

"I am afraid I talked him around, Elizabeth. He has no interest in land, and when I pointed this out, he owned he would much rather buy a better house in London and escape the city in summer by going to Bath. But in truth, will not your sister Jane be more comfortable marrying this summer without Bingley underfoot?"

We subsided into small talk, and on the following day, Mr. Darcy arrived for the sole purpose of securing the harnesses on his carriage horses, handing Mary and me up, and riding escort until we reached the outskirts of London. There, he came to my window, tipped his hat, and with my heart swooning painfully, I went home to Longbourn.

My wedding, set for May 22, caused no small uproar in the neighborhood in which I grew up. That Netherfield Park was ready for my inspection as the future mistress of the place by the eighth of the month only added to the notoriety of my upcoming nuptials. The general interest, the salacious glee of the gossiping matrons who anticipated a great wedding, and even the bustling expectation of the shopkeepers threw my mother into predictable tumult, and thinking to put her mind elsewhere, I took her to see the house—not as a visitor but as mother of its mistress.

Expecting the worst, I was gratified by the sudden change in my mother's demeanor when the great doors opened. She met Mrs. Nichols with a modicum of dignity, and upon going from room to room, looking into cupboards and closets, and picking over the place from top to bottom, she was, for once, ready to be pleased by everything. When we ended in the kitchen, the reason for her complacence became clear because she said with a sly glance at me, "Lizzy, I have been thinking that your wedding breakfast at home will be a terrible squeeze."

I wrote to my intended.

Dear Mr. Darcy,

I am sorry to call you by such a formal appellation still, but having been in love with Mr. Darcy for some while, I do not yet fancy writing a love letter to a stranger named Fitzwilliam.

My news is just what you would expect. Longbourn is very noisy, my father is determined to be contrary about everything, and Mama's nerves are so delicate that we have taken to mixing up jars of a tonic sent to us by Jane's betrothed.

The highlight of this turn is to Jane's benefit, for yesterday, some mention of that 'other' wedding on the fifth of June earned only a dismissive wave of Mama's hand—a trifling by comparison to the spectacle of grandeur we face a fortnight from today.

But that is not the reason for this letter, my love. Mama and I have settled that our wedding breakfast will be held at Netherfield Park, that the thing will need to be 'done up right' if we are to hold up our heads at all. And now it falls to me to assure you that you may safely indulge whatever excesses you wish in regards to Netherfield.

In exchange for these concessions to my mother's requests, I have put forward my fond hope that my aunt Gardiner will serve as your hostess until I am free to take up my place. My thinking is that we shall enjoy a few tolerable entertainments, and hopefully, we shall be spared evenings at Longbourn altogether.

All that remains is to admit that you were very right to purchase Netherfield, though I trust you are too much the gentleman to openly gloat over having won the point.

Your very own devoted fiend,
Elizabeth

Mr. Darcy's Story...

AT LAST! I HAD BEEN GIVEN SOMETHING MEANINGFUL TO DO. SUMMONing my town butler and housekeeper, I barked out a series of orders, and by the day after Elizabeth's letter arrived, three loaded carts went forth from London to Hertfordshire. Thither also went three of my maids, my cook's assistant, and the under-butler, a young man shaping up well who I thought should be given the job of head man at Netherfield.

It was with gratification that a few days thereafter I received another letter from my love. After a tender greeting, she wrote—

Clearly, I did not know what I asked of you, nor did I imagine the depth and breadth of your capacity to provide. Netherfield Park is positively turned upside down and inside out, and my mother has never crowed more loudly of her cleverness in securing you for one of her daughters.

Mr. Thomas, my first butler, is directing the arrangements with deference to my opinion, which in itself is a novelty, and the village is in a high state of readiness on account of the extra work many of our people have secured. You will be greeted in the style of conquering hero when you come to marry me, and if the cottagers' children do not throw flowers in front of your carriage as you progress toward the estate, I shall be very surprised.

But the sugared plum on this cake has been the genius of your management of my father. You would stare to witness his serenity when subjected to Mama's raptures over your excellence. I bow down to you, sir, for you are a wonder…

I smiled in satisfaction, for I had been rather clever with regard to Mr. Bennet. I had found Mr. Gardiner at his office immediately after reading Elizabeth's letter, and together with one of his clerks, we went into the heart of the city. We scouted the second-hand booksellers that abound in certain quarters, and in the space of a few hours, I had amassed a modest haul of books, 320 in all, with which to furnish Netherfield's library. I then sent Mr. Bennet a letter, asking whether he would condescend to look over the collection and direct its placement on the shelves. Flattery was not my strong suit, but I managed to hint at my confidence that he would know best what to do.

In the coming week, I spent my time before leaving for Hertfordshire with my man of business, my banker, and a handful of my London friends. After filling every morning with the necessary work of securing another estate, looking carefully at my accounts, and adjusting my investments to secure them for the future, I went to my club for the afternoons. There I met Lord Cobham and spoke to him for an hour about horses. I also dined on a Wednesday with Creston and

Richardson, known to me from my days at Cambridge, and on the following day, I listened to Charles Middleton's insights with regards to European movements in the colonial world. In all these encounters, I wondered whether they would be my last—whether after *marrying down* in the prevailing wrong-headed sense of things, I would be set aside by men I valued.

The sober fact that I may very well lose friends, I countered with remembrances of Elizabeth Bennet's fiery eyes or the way in which she carried a gown, from her shoulders to the ground. A queen born could not possibly move more gracefully. Then thinking that I must sooner or later see my uncle, I went to his townhouse.

"What is this about Anne?" the earl grumbled at me.

"She has no partiality for me, and I have none for her, sir."

"Partiality! Harrumph! Who has need of partiality in a marriage? But perhaps you could do better."

"Perhaps I could. I hear Langford lost heavily at cards last night."

This constituted the rhythm of my visit. When my uncle brought up the advantageous match he hoped for from me, I countered with some *on dit* I had heard about my cousin, his heir. We parted politely but readily, and I went to see the countess. She too, having heard I had decided against Anne de Bourgh, was in mind of my marriage and what she could get out of it.

"What of Barnstaple's daughter?"

"Who?"

"Eleanor—the young lady I introduced you to at dinner when last you came."

"I am sorry, Aunt. I do not remember her at all. But who are you thinking of for Langford?"

I continued to be stupid when my prospects were brought up and sharply curious of my cousin's fated match. That my aunt was having difficulty finding someone rich enough to help them financially and foolish enough to attach themselves to a spendthrift did not make my probing comfortable for her, and when at last I concluded my call, I felt a little relief that, should they cut me, I would be spared their incessant grasping.

By the time Richard arrived from Pirbright to take me to be married, I was fully and philosophically acquiescent to the consequences of marrying Elizabeth Bennet. The whole lot could go hang if they did not like it, and with that resolution came a lightness of spirit I had not known since childhood.

WE ARRIVED IN HERTFORDSHIRE, AND REFLECTING MY STATE OF newfound liberty, I threw the doors open to the neighborhood. I hosted Sir William Lucas and his family with a sumptuous dinner. The Bennets came too, of course, and Mrs. Gardiner managed to move lightly between the rival matrons by complimenting them by turns.

Elizabeth arrived in an envelope of pale gold silk and smote me anew, and even Richard looked admiringly at her radiant glow.

"Will I do, Mr. Darcy?" she said to me when I managed to pull her away from Georgiana to greet her privately.

"Will you do what, miss? Floor me with your effulgence? I am blinded, my love."

"What do you think of the house?"

"What house?" I asked, still looking into her eyes.

"Your humble country dwelling, sir. The hovel in which you will be required to camp from time to time when rubbing elbows with your rustic relations."

I looked around, and not wishing to betray that it was, in comparison to Pemberley, a very modest house, I commended her taste.

"How are things progressing for your mother's breakfast?" I asked.

"The *potage ala reine* is much discussed, and upon securing a box of pomegranates from your town purveyor, I believe we shall manage to have it made."

"At breakfast?"

"We mean to be ridiculous, Mr. Darcy."

"And the cake?"

"Enormous! Cook says it will soak up half a cask of brandy. And it will be covered in white icing, a wonder in Hertfordshire from the fuss being made. Mama is distressing herself as to how to do the same for Jane."

"You had better tell her to use Netherfield's cook so your sister feels no slight. Might I give them shares in your uncle's business as a wedding gift?"

"My word, but you are open-handed, sir. What next? Will you buy Mama her own carriage?"

"If you would let me."

"Absolutely not! She is becoming intolerable even now. I shall admit to you that I look forward to seeing the downs and, in that clean, astringent air, forgoing this extravagance. I feel slightly tarnished."

"A repairing lease is in order, then," I said, forgetting we were not alone and pushing a little curl off her cheek. "We shall go on a tour of austerity and dine on crusts of bread soaked in ale."

She laughed. "Have you sent horses everywhere?"

"Strings and strings of them."

"And are the innkeepers airing our sheets and polishing the glass?"

I looked at her with the great tenderness I felt and said in perfect imitation of my former self, "Good lord, Elizabeth. I certainly hope so."

She smiled so very softly at me, I wished we were indeed private. "Are you not a little anxious, Mr. Darcy?"

"About marrying you on Friday? No, fiend, I am not anxious at all. Having used up all my nerves in securing your consent, I am unperturbed at the prospect of signing over my worldly goods to you."

"How dull," she said, tipping her head to the side and looking at me.

"Dull! How can you say so? I am for once unruffled."

"But I enjoy ruffling you."

I could not quite restrain the lusty note in my chuckle when I said, "Believe me, Elizabeth, you will ruffle me very well come Friday night."

I SECURED MY BRIDE ON A DAY THAT STARTED WET BUT CLEARED delightfully. For the most part, I stood mutely to one side, for after saying, "I do," and "I will," I was of little use to anybody. My wife—the thrill of calling her this has not yet subsided—stood as though in a light from above, and as always, she drew people to her, moths to the flame. With my sister standing at her side, Elizabeth greeted her neighbors warmly, teased her friends with a lightness of touch that made her everyone's favorite, and cajoled her sisters with master strokes of jokes, admonishments, and demonstrations of tenderness. She ended by receiving her father with a look ripe with both affection and irony.

"Well, Papa, I am no longer crossed in love. You will need to find a new favorite among your daughters. I suggest Kitty, for even you will own that she could be more than she is."

"But I am busy with your library," he said with a twinkle.

"Make Kitty help you, sir, and while she is setting books on the shelves, tell her about *Ivanhoe*."

Mr. Bennet kissed her cheek. "I am glad you are going away, Lizzy, for I have a strong suspicion your new position as Mrs. Darcy will give you notions of managing *me*."

Mrs. Bennet then pushed herself forward and threw herself on her newly crowned *dearest daughter*. Over the lady's shoulder, Elizabeth's eyes ruefully met mine, and I came forward.

"I have never attended a better wedding breakfast, Mrs. Bennet," I said truthfully. "You have outdone yourself. Might I," I said, after brushing her hand with my lips, "beg leave to steal your daughter?"

AS THE NOTICE OF MY SHOCKING WEDDING CIRCULATED LONDON, Elizabeth and I walked for miles along chalk-colored paths amidst tufts of rye grass. Closer to the coast, she could rarely take her eyes from the waves. Whether they appeared as folds of blue velvet serenely breathing or fractured white tops pounding the shingle, she marveled at their power. And in taking Elizabeth to see things I had observed many times, I saw everything anew. For once, I felt gratitude where I had only felt entitlement, and our simple movements—breakfast, walking, a carriage ride to another inn, passionate afternoons, a cozy supper in a fire-lit room, reading, midnight conversations—all these ordinary things, done with Elizabeth, rejuvenated my soul.

I had longed for this union, and yet I had no notion that Elizabeth's delight would ignite such joy within me. By degrees I began to allow myself to speak unguardedly, to unshackle the tightly controlled inner man. Lying in a linen shift with one shoulder bared and her hair spilling in waves over my chest, my young wife listened to me with compassion, with commiseration, and upon occasion, with a chuckle as I unburdened myself of my ponderous history. Not only had I secured her love, I had earned her friendship, and this was the most humbling gift she could have given me.

UPON OUR RETURN TO NETHERFIELD, RICHARD CAME DOWN THE steps, and standing aside so Elizabeth could be scooped up by Georgiana, Mary, and Jane, he looked me up and down.

"I do not recognize you, Darcy," he said. "What has happened to your face?"

"I have laughed more in two weeks than I have in twenty years," I said. "I believe my jaw is realigned."

"You inspire me, Darcy."

"To marry?"

"Certainly to marry for affection," he said lightly.

We saw Jane married two days later, and on our last night before leaving for Pemberley, we had a family supper at Netherfield.

In the parlor, Mrs. Bennet beckoned me and said, "Mr. Darcy, do you not think that my daughters Kitty and Lydia would take in London?"

My wife stiffened, but for once I knew what to do. I sat down next to her mother and said, at my most obliging, "Mrs. Bennet—Mother Bennet—may I call you that? I would, of course, oblige you by presenting them when they are made presentable."

"Made presentable?" Her eyes darted to her daughters and raked over them as they sat whispering in the corner as though searching for some flaw in their hair or their dresses.

"I have not discussed the recommended course with Elizabeth, you understand, and her opinion of what is to be done about them must stand over anything I might think of."

She bristled. "What is to be done about them?"

"They are perfectly behaved for the country, Mother Bennet, but in town they would be deemed—"

"Fast," Elizabeth cut in sharply.

I patted Mrs. Bennet's hand reassuringly. "If you would like, I can send to you a lady of my acquaintance, a Lady Charlotte Wainright. She was married to an admiral and is fourth daughter of the Duke of Leinster. She is considered an authority on what constitutes town manners and would put in a word about vouchers at Almack's if she thought that Kitty and Lydia would take. Well, you and Elizabeth should consider the matter and decide what is best. Meanwhile, I have been meaning to ask whether you would like my workers to make any trifling repairs at Longbourn before I send them back to London. I believe they are nearly finished at Netherfield."

THAT EVENING WE RETIRED EARLY. I SLIPPED INTO ELIZABETH'S ROOM, as I did every night, for the pleasure of watching her brush her hair.

"Mother Bennet?" she asked archly.

"Of what do you wish to accuse me, Elizabeth?"

"I think it churlish of you to make me love you for your brusqueness.

only *now* to come the charmer."

I came up behind her and took up her brush. With endless fascination, I stroked through the silken strands on her head, losing myself in the rhythm and the feel of this nightly ritual.

"And who is this Lady Charlotte?" she asked, looking up at me in the mirror with a tiny frown and pulling me out of my distraction.

"She is exactly who you imagine her to be, love."

"Horrible, in fact."

"Yes."

"And you think she might do my sisters some good?"

"I do not rightly know, but she regularly refers young ladies to the rigors of a Swiss school where they are taken away from everyone and everything they know and indoctrinated with a good deal of fashionable nonsense."

"Such as?"

"Such as the classic accomplishments. Caroline Bingley is a product of that brand of education. Do not shudder, fiend. She went in with her basic nature, which was sniping and grasping, and she came out with it intact but lacquered over. I doubt very much they could dampen Lydia's high spirits, but perhaps they might be directed into more suitable channels. Kitty might polish well, however."

My wife heaved a great sigh, so I put down the brush and began to tenderly kiss her ear. "We do not have to decide anything today," I whispered before proceeding to turn her thoughts in another direction altogether.

In the morning, we left Hertfordshire. I thought my Elizabeth might be sad, but she was in fact only reflective, and by degrees over that three-day journey, we became truly bound to one another. The proximity, together with the discomfort, confinement, and unending boredom of such a journey, rubbed us together in more ways than the physical. Soon enough, we were ground down where we met as a couple, polished to perfectly fit one with the other, and infinitely comfortable.

Richard came with us as far as Bedford before peeling off to visit some friends in Cambridge and then circling back to the Brigade of Guards in Surrey. He kept Georgiana and Mary occupied in my sister's carriage.

The three of them ran shy of us, disinclined to join us in our coach save for a few short legs. When I hinted my bewilderment at this stand-offishness, Richard laughed. "Darcy, neither of you has eyes for anyone else. In time, I hope, you will have room to spare for the rest of us."

"I do not mean to be—"

"Of course you do not, but you are. Now, I have a packet of letters for you that we agreed I would hold until now."

At Bedford, Richard handed over my post that, aside from letters from my steward and man of business, I had purposely refused to read. With a jaundiced eye, I looked at the alarming pile wrapped in string.

"Take heart, Cousin," Richard said cheerfully, "for they cannot *all* be damning, and you have only to reflect on your current happiness to know that much of this is meaningless."

Upon rejoining Elizabeth in the coach after our stop in Bedford, she said, "You had better tell me what has put that grave look upon your face, Willum."

My mother called me 'Willum,' and when I shared this small intimacy from my boyhood, Elizabeth decided she would call me that as well. The sound of my mother's pet name never failed to soften me, and so I heaved a great sigh and put the stack of letters between us.

"You have finally decided you must face the world's opinion, then? Would you like me to read them to you?"

"On no account. The things that might be said of you—"

"—I can bear with a great deal of amusement, I assure you. Besides, what else is there for us to do? I begin to think Pemberley is a place in some mystical future and that we shall be forever on the road to meet her. Now, let us tackle Black Annis first, shall we? After what we hear from *her*, what anyone else cares to say will hardly signify."

In consequence of my wife's inclination to be joyful, a distasteful duty produced instead a great deal of laughter. We took turns reading in various voices mimicking our correspondents, whether it was my tremulous vibrato of the countess's shock and dismay, or Elizabeth's gruff barks of outrage from the earl. My friends couched tepid congratulations in the language of commiseration, and when I said, "My love, they one and all believe I have gotten some country squire's daughter with child," she looked her delight.

"Do they?" she cried.

"Of a certainty. These letters are written as condolences for consequences that must earn their sympathy."

"How do you know, Mr. Darcy?"

"You know very well how I know, fiend. I have had to write one or two of those grievous congratulations myself. Let us see what my banker says."

My professional acquaintances sent best wishes composed strictly for the sake of form, none knowing whether they would somehow benefit or suffer from my unaccountable wedding.

We also read all the society notices.

Mr. D of Derbyshire has confounded all his brethren by publishing notice of his wedding to a Miss B of Hertfordshire two days ago.

Lord and Lady M have taken the knocker from their door for reasons thought to be related to the surprise wedding of their nephew.

But by far, Lady Catherine's letter was the most absorbing, for she managed five full pages of such a deranged rant that anyone reading it must either go mad or be well entertained. One entire page was spent on my legal recourse to dissolve an illegal marriage, and another page dwelt in graphic detail on the stains of scandal for which my temptress must pay with an eternity in hell.

After we had torn these letters into tiny bits and strewn them over twenty miles of muddy road, I took Elizabeth in my arms and held her close while we dozed.

When I awoke, I said, "Elizabeth, do you know I have never been happier?"

"Even after all those dreadful letters?" she asked on a yawn.

"Particularly after all those dreadful letters. Whoever comes to Pemberley now, whoever writes to me or wishes to know me, will do so from simpler motives. I had not realized what tension I suffered from having to discern what everyone wanted of me."

"Do you know what I want from you?" she asked, but before I could come to a salacious conclusion, she said, "I want a very, very long walk."

In consequence, the next day when we came to the perimeter of Pemberley's park, I knocked on the roof of the coach and sent the whole cavalcade forward. Taking my wife's hand, we walked three miles to the rise overlooking my house, and stopping to stare, she said in a voice of wonder, "Is this home, Willum?"

Suddenly Pemberley was no longer a legacy to me. It was just a house! I wished to laugh aloud at my lifelong obsession with what was only, in essence, a place to eat and sleep, but instead I said, "Where you are is home to me, Elizabeth. Will you stay here with me?"

My love does not like me sinking into maudlin sentiment. She wrinkled her nose and sighed reprovingly. "It is very grand."

"Would you rather have a cottage, my love? We can have Lady Catherine's advisors begin to dissolve our contract. I shall put you on the edge of the estate in a stodgy little place where you can bear my love children, and I shall send you a guinea every so often."

"Will I get a ham at Christmas?"

"Lord! What next?" I huffed. "Am I to buy silver buckles for your shoes?"

"Certainly after every boy child," she said with a sniff.

And so we went down the rise to the house where the staff had flung open the doors to welcome us home.

Epilogue

Elizabeth's Story...

It falls to me, I suppose, to tell what has since transpired. In the end, Pemberley suited me infinitely well, and we did not resort to a dissolution of our marriage so that I could inhabit a moldy cottage. The fortunes of our friends, acquaintances, and relations, however, were variable.

Of those who did not fare well, George Wickham must be first on the list. He contracted a tropical fever and died one week after landing in Jamaica. I must also report that my husband's cousin, Lord Langford, not only lost heavily at cards, but he lost heavily with regards to his future. Desperate to bolster the family fortunes, the Earl of Matlock arranged with his sister, Lady Catherine, to marry his son to her daughter, Anne, and combine the income of Rosings Park with that of Matlock.

But Lord Langford had enjoyed the services of the most celebrated Cyprians in London and had some very particular notions about what he deserved in a wife. Upon seeing Anne, a girl he had not laid eyes on for more than seven years, Langford also went straight to Jamaica.

He writes he has no intention to return until such time as he is earl. Meanwhile, he *married* a girl named Jenny of no parentage at all, making Darcy's marriage to me a staid bow to convention by comparison.

Lord and Lady Matlock could not quite continue to be important figures in a society that laughed behind its hand at the shocking desertion of their heir. After only a few faint snubs, they removed to their country house and are rumored to be in a full scale of retrenchment that precludes their entertaining anybody.

Mr. Collins never did regain the total approbation of his noble patroness. He had, after all, brought the viper to her bosom, and in consequence, she barely tolerated him. In turn, he became insufferable to live with, and Charlotte has since gone to live at Longbourn with my mother. That convoluted tale would take far too long to enumerate, but suffice it to say, they get on remarkably well for two people so opposite in nature.

My sisters Lydia and Kitty were sent off to be *finished* in Switzerland. Lydia, of course, did not return finished at all. In fact, she did not return to England, having married a German count with more flash than substance. Her letters are haphazard at best, and she swings from gay descriptions of going from one glamorous party after another to broad hints for money. Kitty, by contrast, returned as polished as any debutante could be, and we brought her out in a modest way, which suited our distaste for hectic town life. But for all her newfound sophistication, her country upbringing would prevail, and after two abbreviated Seasons, she returned to Meryton and promptly fell in love with John Lucas!

Georgiana managed a somewhat awkward debut. We had returned to town a few months after our shocking *elopement* as it has since been styled, and we were treated with such uneven and occasionally outright false politeness from society that her ball was attended by only twenty-two couples. Mr. Darcy's friends, Lord Cobham, Mr. Creston, and Mr. Richardson, came and gamely danced the entire night with her.

That they covertly looked me over from head to foot did not bother me in the least, for I had no belly to satisfy their curiosity, and the fact that my husband very publicly adored me put much of everyone else's speculation to rest. By the following Season, the prevailing wisdom of the *bon ton* had turned our shameful elopement into a love match.

A love match has so far eluded Charles Bingley. He lives the town life with the limpets of Mr. Hurst, Mrs. Hurst, and Miss Bingley still firmly attached. Willum says he sometimes thinks Bingley is waiting for Mr. Bromley to fall ill from one of his patients so he can have Jane as a widow. I reply that Caroline Bingley is very hopeful I shall die in childbed so she can have my husband.

Georgiana has remained at home with us, and she exhibits no inclination to find a husband. In this we are fully supportive, for if she has a life she enjoys and is surrounded by people who love her, why should she leave?

My sister Jane did learn to make jam, and we have just opened a jar sent to Pemberley from her kitchen. She is serenely happy being Robert Bromley's support in a life full of people who need his attention. They have the happy advantage of being close enough to visit Aunt and Uncle Gardiner any day of the week, and I hardly read a letter from Jane in which some mention is not made of a family party. This year, they are coming to Pemberley for Christmas, and though I know they will enjoy themselves, I have no doubt that half the people on the estate will seek out Mr. Bromley for some remedy or cure.

However intriguing the vagaries of fate when observed from the distance of time, they are eclipsed by the reversal of fortune enjoyed by my sister Mary. She traveled to Pemberley with us after our wedding, and when we returned to London for Georgiana's debut, she went to stay with Jane who, newly married herself and immersed in the strange world of medical life, was all at sea. Between the two of them, they learned to manage an establishment that was both a home and a medical office.

The day for them, as I understand it, begins with an early breakfast and the management of household business compressed into the hour before the doorknocker begins to sound. Thereafter, they greet various persons, make them comfortable in a small parlor, and show them into the consultation room when Mr. Bromley is finished with the patient he attended just before.

This seemed a simple affair to me, but nothing is simple when dealing with persons who are sick. There were those who had to be helped up and down the stairs, those who needed to be listened to, and those who had endless—often imaginary—complaints that required an attitude of concerned interest. Occasionally, someone would arrive in such a dire state of either disability or injury that an upstairs room, set aside for the purpose, would be opened. There, the patient would stay until they could be safely moved—either to their home or to the undertaker. These sudden emergencies threw the whole house into a tumult. In all cases, this general bustle was a world away from the simple life of a country squire's daughter.

After the last patient is seen out the door, tea will be called for, and after Mr. Bromley forces down a few sandwiches and cakes, he will leave for an afternoon of traversing half of London to see to his homebound patients. Then there commences the work of running a gentleman's modest house that, in truth, requires a great deal of effort since they can hardly afford an army of servants. Throughout this period, Jane has adjusted to a life with a tenth of the leisure she was used to, and Mary, thoroughly occupied, has thrived.

My middle sister might very well still be there as a spinster were it not for the arrival of a wounded man, half carried up the steps by an alarmingly large soldier named Sergeant Brown.

"Colonel Fitzwilliam!" Mary cried out, and with tears streaming down her face, she went to him.

Grimacing a brave smile, he winked at her and said, "Mary Bennet, what a delight to see you again."

While supervising the movement of artillery from Pirbright to the Hyde Park Barracks, an ordinance exploded just outside Richmond, killing three men and wounding half a dozen more, Colonel Fitzwilliam among them. Feeling himself more fortunate than the rest, with *only three shards* of molten metal in his shoulder and back, Richard declined the medical services of the brigade doctor who approached him with bloody sleeves.

With a makeshift bandage and a bottle of brandy, he directed his batman to take him straight to Bromley in London. He later joked that, if a sawbones were going to finish him off, he would prefer it be someone he knew. The truth was that he very nearly died, but after surviving a harrowing fever, he convalesced in the doctor's sick room and credits my sister's assiduous care with his survival.

The recovery for Richard was long and fraught, but in the midst of the difficulty, he realized that no woman in the world made him feel more comfortable or more at ease than my sister. And Mary, who had been in love with my husband's cousin almost from the very first moment of seeing him, willed him to live by means of her considerable and intense devotion to his care.

As he gradually became well, Colonel Fitzwilliam began to go downstairs to dinner with the family, to sit in the parlor, and to think on settling into a comfortable life much like that enjoyed by Jane and Robert Bromley. He wrote to Darcy, and in a few months, he sold his commission, confessed his undying love to Mary, and after a simple ceremony, took her to Staffordshire.

There, he bought her a pretty little house where she set up a kitchen garden and made herself endlessly useful. Richard, having been wounded and suffering a loss of the full function of his shoulder, decided he would rather find a business that could support wounded soldiers than passively work the land, and so he bought Mr. Bingley's last pottery factory—amiably priced on account of their friendship— with this aim in mind.

The giant, Sergeant Brown, did not go to Staffordshire. He had stayed at Mr. Bromley's house while caring for his colonel. He was called upon to assist with patients from time to time, and in doing so, he developed an interest in doing something other than soldiering. Because of his brute strength and sheer size, he became an expert bone setter as well as my brother-in-law's factotum. Between them, they became known for their work with joints and bones, and they hired rooms in Harley Street. And Jane, heavily with child, was glad to call quits. She quietly set about hiring a nurse to take over her public duties and to see to the relocation of the workplace to a site somewhere removed from her parlor. When last I visited, she looked less careworn and more beautifully serene than ever.

I SAT UP IN BED, AND AFTER ASKING FOR THE CURTAINS TO BE OPENED to a brilliantly lit day, my husband came quietly into the room as the maid slipped quietly out.

"Is she sleeping?" he asked in a tender whisper. How many times have we melted over an infant—an animal, a niece, a nephew, or one of our own?

"Not for long," I whispered back. "She is a loud one, I am afraid."

He carefully sat next to me and kissed my hand. "Assure me you are well, love," he said.

"Caroline Bingley will not get you this time, sir."

"She will not get me any time."

He pushed a few strands of hair from my forehead, causing the breath to catch in my throat. He still has the capacity to make me feel infinitely loved.

After a moment of silent reflection, he said, "Robert tells me he has never known a woman to have an easier time of it than you, but I confess, I hate the sound of my children being born."

"Like your daughter, I am not quiet," I said with a low chuckle. "But what is this?"

He handed me a small box, and I opened it to see two finely crafted silver buckles. This is our ritual, and after four darling raven-haired babies, I now have a collection. As with each set, they will be engraved and given to our love children.

"We are like these buckles," my husband mused as he stared helplessly at the silver baubles and then at his first daughter.

When I looked up at him questioningly, he said simply, "A matched pair, my fiend." He kissed the palm of my hand. "Now rest, Elizabeth. There is a houseful of people who want to come see you, and I shall not share you until you have slept for half the day at least."

I stifled the urge to kiss his hand. My husband is easily undone by such demonstrations of worship. Instead, I said, "I would rather not be alone just now. Will you bring a chair close and bear me company?"

A look of great tenderness stole over his face, and I could no longer resist. I kissed his hand and fell into a peaceful rest, secure in the knowledge he would be there when I awoke on this special day and always.

Acknowledgments

M any thanks to the Meryton Press team. From day one, everyone has been consistently helpful, patient, and so accommodating. A special thanks to my editors, Debbie Styne and Ellen Pickels, who applied their genius to my offering, as well as Janet Taylor, whose help and encouragement have been invaluable throughout.

About the Author

Photography by Zach Fisher

In addition to mosaic art, which she creates at Studio Luminaria (her home-based glass shop in El Paso, Texas), Grace enjoys writing Regency romance and Pride and Prejudice variations.

Lightning Source UK Ltd.
Milton Keynes UK
UKHW010640040321
379777UK00001B/60